Tracks in the Straw

TALES SPUN FROM THE MANGER

by Ted Loder

Drawings by Ed Kerns

LuraMedia™

Also by Ted Loder:
  EAVESDROPPING ON THE ECHOES:
  Voices from the Old Testament

  GUERRILLAS OF GRACE:
  Prayers for the Battle

  NO ONE BUT US:
  Personal Reflections on Public Sanctuary

  WRESTLING THE LIGHT:
  Ache and Awe in the Human-Divine Struggle

LuraMedia
7060 Miramar Road, Suite 104
San Diego, CA 92121

Library of Congress Cataloging-in-Publication Data
Loder, Ted, date.
    Tracks in the straw.
    Summary: A collection of stories centering on the birth
of Jesus.
    1. Jesus Christ—Fiction. 2. Christmas stories.
[1. Jesus Christ—Fiction. 2. Christmas—Fiction. 3. Short stories]
I. Kerns, Ed., ill.   II. Title.
PS3562.0296T7   1985   813'.54 [Fic]   85-23046
ISBN 0-931055-06-7

For Mark, David, Karen, and Thomas
whose stories are wondrous
and whose tracks are in my heart.

Contents

Naked Isn't the Last Straw

UNBORN: **B**ut why me?

ANGEL: I don't know. Why not you? No doubt there's a reason. You'll find out.

UNBORN: Oh, do I have to do it? It sounds just awful! What does it mean to get born, anyway?

ANGEL: Getting born is . . . well, it's entering a new place, a different place from where you are. And you have to become very small to get in. That's the way it's designed. There's no other way to do it. You have to start as a baby.

UNBORN: Baby? What's a baby?

ANGEL: A baby is a very tiny creature. At first they're quite
            helpless. Oh, they have all the parts they'll have when
            they get bigger and stronger, only none of the parts
            works very well. Except certain ones. You'll see.

UNBORN: Helpless? Oh, I *know* I won't like it. I don't want to
            do it!

ANGEL: Someone will be there to take care of you, probably.

UNBORN: *(Slightly panicked)* Probably? *Probably* someone
            will?

ANGEL: Well, usually. Your mother and father, usually.

UNBORN: What are they?

ANGEL: Mothers and fathers? Well, they are . . . like other
            human beings. Only they aren't quite like each other.
            If they were, there wouldn't be babies.

UNBORN: Ich! It sounds worse all the time. I'm just not doing it.
            Besides, what are human beings?

ANGEL: Well, I'm not sure what to tell you about them. They
            are creatures pretty much like all the other creatures
            God made. Only they are little more . . . complicated,
            shall we say. They eat and sleep and walk around and
            have sex and babies. And they fight a lot over eating
            and sex, and who can walk or sleep where, and whose
            babies have what rights. But they think, too, some-
            times. And they love, once in a while, until it begins to
            scare them. They create things, and they destroy
            things. They struggle. Oh, yes! They certainly struggle.
            They are quite unpredictable, really, which means of
            course, that they are free. And they keep looking for
            God . . . sort of.

UNBORN: Sort of? What does *that* mean?

ANGEL: Well, they can't seem to decide about it, really. They
            don't seem to know what they fear most: that they
            won't find God or that they *will*. So they "sort of"
            look, without concentrating much on how or where or
            even what they're looking for. But they don't seem
            quite able to stop looking either, especially when they
            are afraid, which is often. Only they don't like to

admit it. So they pretend a lot.

UNBORN: Oh, I knew it. I just *knew* it! They sound terribly complicated. And confused. I don't want to be born at all ... Does it hurt, being born?

ANGEL: Some, at first, while you're getting into the world.

UNBORN: Then it's over?

ANGEL: Not exactly. Sometimes it hurts more later on. There are different kinds of hurt. That's partly what I mean about human beings being complicated.

UNBORN: But why are they so complicated?

ANGEL: Oh, I don't know. Some say it's because of sin. They say human beings messed things up. And maybe that's partly true.

UNBORN: Partly?

ANGEL: Well, yes. I think they are *meant* to be complicated, too. I think God created them that way. It's part of all those possibilities God put into them. I guess you'll be finding out, won't you?

UNBORN: It sounds so hard. Is there any hope for human beings?

ANGEL: Yes. Oh, yes! There . . . certainly is. You'll see.

UNBORN: I'm not going to like it at all. I'm going to apply for an exemption.

ANGEL: But you will like it! Really. Human beings are beautiful, too. And so is the earth.

UNBORN: Earth? What's the earth? Is it like here?

ANGEL: Sometimes it is. But mostly, not very. Earth is the home of human beings. It's where they live, or at least try to.

UNBORN: Where is it?

ANGEL: Come here . . . look . . . where I'm pointing. See . . . way, way over there, as far as you can see across thousands of light years . . . there, that little speck of blue. That's it. Can you make it out?

UNBORN: Barely . . . I don't have to go yet, do I?

ANGEL: Well . . . not yet. There *is* something else I must tell you

	before you get born.
UNBORN:	Oh, do you have to? I'm already so confused and scared. Do you have to tell me more?
ANGEL:	Yes, it's important.
UNBORN:	Is it good or bad? I don't want to hear any more bad things!
ANGEL:	I didn't think I'd told you anything that's bad. I told you some hard things about being a human being. But I didn't mean to make them sound bad. I'm sorry if I did.
UNBORN:	Well, they sounded bad to me—all that stuff about human beings being complicated and fighting about things. And what you said about it sometimes hurting more *after* you're born than while you're being born. Isn't that bad?
ANGEL:	To an extent, I suppose. But so much of that is just part of the way God makes human beings free by putting so many possibilities in them. Anyway, I don't think what I have to tell you now is either good or bad. It's just necessary.
UNBORN:	All right, what is it?
ANGEL:	It's that sometime while you are waiting to be born, you start forgetting. By the time you're actually born, you will have forgotten everything . . . or almost everything.
UNBORN:	What do you mean, I'll have forgotten? Forgotten *what?*
ANGEL:	You will have forgotten everything we've talked about. You won't remember me or even having been here.
UNBORN:	I won't remember anything? *Nothing?* None of the secrets? Oh, that sounds bad to me. In fact, it sounds terrible.
ANGEL:	But it really isn't. You see, if you did remember, you wouldn't really be entirely human. If you remembered, you wouldn't take your life "there" seriously. You might think it didn't matter. And it does. It mat-

ters urgently. So you forget "here." Oh, from time to time in the years after you're born, you'll have certain feelings that you won't quite understand: certain longings, tugs, strange periods of restlessness. You'll wonder about them! And there will be moments when something will suddenly stir and pass over your soul, like a breeze over water, causing just the very slightest ripple. Then it will be gone, leaving a curious residue of sadness and joy in you. Those will be hints. But you won't remember anything specific about here and us.

UNBORN: *(Urgently)* But I can come back here, can't I? When I'm done being human, can't I get born back here?

ANGEL: Not really. You see, things change, move on. Here won't really be *here* then. I will change. And you'll change. Being human will change you. Very profoundly.

UNBORN: *(Beginning to cry)* Oh, it's awful to have to get born. It's just awful having to leave and never coming back here. It's a terrible loss.

ANGEL: Oh, no. Not really. Actually, it's a gain. I wish I could make you understand, but I can't. Besides, you'd soon forget even if I could make you understand. *(Speaking almost to self)* "Thou hast made human beings little less than God ... Thou hast given them dominion over the works of thy hands ..." Sometimes I wish I ...

UNBORN: What are you saying?

ANGEL: Nothing! Well, actually, I am saying something. I'm saying that to be a human being is a wonder greater than the stars.

UNBORN: But will I always be a human being after I'm born? Will I live on the earth forever?

ANGEL: *(Chuckling)* So many questions! Of course, all of us are creatures, except God. God is the creator. So in some way, yes, you'll always be a human being after you are born. But, no, you will not live on the earth forever.

UNBORN: Oh, you never make things clear. You always muddle them up. If I'm not on the earth forever, then what will happen to me? What *does* happen to human beings if they don't stay on the earth?

ANGEL: Well, that's even harder to explain than trying to tell you what it means to be born. You see, time passes, and . . .

UNBORN: No, I don't see. What's time?

ANGEL: Come here. Look . . . do you see that galaxy whirling over there? It's moving, isn't it?

UNBORN: Of course. Anyone can see that!

ANGEL: Well, for that galaxy to move from the place it *was* to the place it *will be* takes time. That's the way it is with everything. Time measures movement and movement measures time. Understand?

UNBORN: No! I don't understand. Not at all. Besides, what does that have to do with what happens to human beings?

ANGEL: Well, human beings move, too. They move from where they were to where they're going. They move from birth on through days and nights, through all kinds of experiences and struggles. Time measures their movement. They get older as they move. After a while, they move to the end of their time, each one of them. Some have more time to move through than others. But finally, everyone comes to the end of their time. And then they die. Their bodies stop working. They have no more days and nights then.

UNBORN: Die? Is it hard to die?

ANGEL: It seems to be. No matter when a person dies, it seems to be hard. Human beings are usually quite afraid of dying. They wonder about it. They struggle over it long before their time actually ends. When it comes to dying, they are a little like you are about being born. They worry a lot about what will happen to them.

UNBORN: Well, what *does* happen to them?

ANGEL: I can't tell you. Besides, if I told you, you'd forget anyway. What I can tell you is that human beings are not accidents. God planned them.

UNBORN: Oh, the whole business of getting born and being human seems so hard. Why did God have to make it that way?

ANGEL: I'm really not sure. I've thought several eons about it, and I don't think God *had* to make it that way. God just *did* make it that way. So I think it has something to do with love. In some ways love seems to be the hardest lesson of all for human beings.

UNBORN: But love's the best thing there is!

ANGEL: Yes. You and I know that. One day maybe they'll learn, too. Sometimes I ache for the earth whirling around that star over there. It looks so small and fragile, doesn't it?

UNBORN: Yes . . . and I admit it does look beautiful, at least from here. And so quiet. I like quiet. Is it quiet on the earth?

ANGEL: Sometimes. Quiet is another thing that human beings have trouble with . . .

UNBORN: Don't they know about listening?

ANGEL: A little. But they aren't too sure what to listen for when it's quiet. Or even when it's not quiet, for that matter. They miss things, even when they hear them.

UNBORN: And you said I'll forget, too. That's sad.

ANGEL: Sometimes you'll almost remember.

UNBORN: How will I? Can't you tell me?

ANGEL: Well, sometimes when it's a little quiet, mothers and fathers listen to a baby's heartbeat before the baby is born.

UNBORN: They can do that?

ANGEL: Oh, yes!

UNBORN: What does it sound like?

ANGEL: It sounds like the heart of God. Remember that, if you can . . . You will remember that, a little somehow. Well, I think you're about ready to go, don't you? We've covered about everything.

UNBORN: Ready? I still have a million questions. Besides, I haven't even packed yet.

ANGEL: You don't have to pack. You can't take anything with you, anyway.

UNBORN: I can't? Nothing? Not a *thing?*

ANGEL: Nothing.

UNBORN: But I have to have something to wear. I can't get born looking like this!

ANGEL: Believe me, you don't need to take a thing. Whatever you need to wear will be provided for you when you get there.

UNBORN: But I have to make an entrance, don't I? I have to have something to arrive in.

ANGEL: No, you don't.

UNBORN: Now wait just a whirl or two. I don't get to take a stitch with me?

ANGEL: Not a stitch.

UNBORN: *(With agitation)* You mean to tell me that to get born on earth, you not only have to forget everything you ever learned here, AND become small and helpless, AND risk being taken care of by human beings who are complicated and confused, AND survive with people who aren't too sure how to love or even know what love is, AND who fight a lot about things, AND are afraid most of the time, AND get old and die and worry about it, but, to top it all off, you have to start out being absolutely, positively, completely stark naked? HAS ANYONE SPOKEN TO GOD ABOUT THIS? NAKED IS THE LAST STRAW!

ANGEL: Really? Why?

UNBORN: *(With exasperation)* WHY? Tell me, are there people around when you get born?

ANGEL: Of course! Your mother is there, and almost always several others are present.

UNBORN: Well?

ANGEL: Well, what?

UNBORN: Well, so much for going naked, is what! I mean what do human beings think about naked? What'll they think when I whoosh in wearing my basic nothing? It'll be embarrassing, won't it? Sure it will!

ANGEL: Oh, I begin to see the problem. You do learn quickly, don't you?

UNBORN: You bet your sweet Milky Way. If human beings are so uptight about everything, I can just guess how they'll be about my being naked.

ANGEL: Now just wait a whirl or two yourself. In the first place, when you're a baby, nakedness is fine. In fact, they think it's adorable. It's only later that it's a problem.

UNBORN: Okay, try to explain that. Oh, don't bother. I already know, "It's complicated."

ANGEL: But it IS complicated. Sometimes it's even a little funny. You see, when you're a baby, nakedness is fine because . . . well, because to them, a baby's body is beautiful. They love it. They love to hold it, touch it, kiss it, smell it. It seems to remind them of something they've forgotten.

UNBORN: Forgotten? Oh . . . but later on, human bodies turn ugly? Is that it? You mean when you get big, your body isn't beautiful anymore?

ANGEL: No, that isn't exactly it.

UNBORN: For once, could you tell me exactly what it IS?

ANGEL: It really is hard to explain. Maybe the simplest way is to say that it has something to do with the way people learn to think of themselves.

UNBORN: You won't be surprised if I tell you I don't follow that at all.

ANGEL: Well, listen. Almost no human being ever thinks his or her body is what they wish it was after they grow bigger. They think their body is never quite beautiful or strong or handsome enough; or thin or tall or coordinated enough. They always think their nose is too big or their ears stick out, or their eyes are the wrong color or are too close to each other or too far apart; or their chin is weak or their hair is too thin; or their chest is too flat or their neck is too short; or their ankles are too thick, and so on and on and on. And to make it worse, there are things about how God made their bodies work that embarrass them, so they're always either making jokes or frowning about how their bodies work.

UNBORN: Hold on. You are talking about more than bodies here, aren't you? What are you saying?

ANGEL: I'm trying to say that it isn't just their bodies that they are referring to when they think and talk that way. They are really talking about how they feel about themselves as human beings, as individual persons. They're really talking about things that frighten them —like sex, or being laughed at, or being humiliated, or not being liked, or being thought stupid. Or they're really talking about how it is to get old and die—all those things that make them feel that maybe there's something wrong with them and they aren't worth much somehow.

UNBORN: But . . . if God made human beings that way, why . . . are they . . . I mean why, when they see a baby, don't they . . . remember?

ANGEL: Well, I think what it comes down to is, human beings have trouble accepting themselves as God's creatures. Deep down they think somehow it's bad to be a creature. Strangely, they think maybe other people won't like them very much because of that. And most deeply, they don't seem to like themselves much because of that. So they make it hard for themselves and each other. They hide. They hide behind clothes, behind all sorts of poses, masks, deceptions, pretenses. They even hide behind their race or nationality. Much of the time they hide behind religion, many of them. They try to make gods of themselves. Oh, it is so hard to explain. But you'll see.

UNBORN: *(Pausing)* It sounds so lonely.

ANGEL: Yes. It is. But you see, it's more lonely because of what

	human beings do about their loneliness.
UNBORN:	You always muddle things all up. What do you mean now?
ANGEL:	I mean that, partly, human beings are created lonely by God. In a way, feeling lonely is almost a way of remembering here. It's like a wind ripple on the water. And lonely is also the result of each human being created as an individual, as a particular person not quite like any other; no person can feel or think or decide for another, finally.
UNBORN:	Human beings can do all that for themselves? I mean, feel . . . think . . . decide?
ANGEL:	They can and do, no matter how much they protest, or blame others, or want others to do it for them. You'll always be lonely because you are free. But you just become more lonely if you do things to try to make yourself less lonely. Do you understand?
UNBORN:	No, not really. But I suppose I'll learn after I'm born. I wish, after I'm born, I could remember all you said.
ANGEL:	Just try not to be afraid of loneliness. Listen to it. In a way, loneliness is like nakedness. Both have to do with being a creature and accepting who you are. Loneliness is remembering.
UNBORN:	I'm not sure I understand . . . But anyway, I guess I'm as ready to go as I'll ever be. Will you come and visit me on earth?
ANGEL:	Oh, yes. There are always many of us around. All the time, everywhere.
UNBORN:	Well, that's good. At least that makes me feel a little better about going.
ANGEL:	The only thing is that when I visit, I won't seem to you anything like who I really am.
UNBORN:	You won't?
ANGEL:	No. Because God is never obvious. If God was obvious, human beings wouldn't be free. They'd *have* to respond. Unless love is freely given, it wouldn't mean anything. And love is what matters to God. You know

that, don't you?

UNBORN: I think so. But I feel as if I'm already beginning to forget. How will I know when you visit? Hurry! Tell me.

ANGEL: You won't know, directly. It won't be obvious, as I said. Besides, the strange thing is that in spite of their conflicts about bodies, human beings have trouble recognizing or believing in anything that doesn't have a body they can see and measure. God keeps sending all sorts of ingenious messages and messengers, but human beings don't seem to make any connections between the messages and God. Mostly, they don't even pay much attention to the messages. Sometimes, some do. Maybe you will be one who does. But anyway, I *will* visit you.

UNBORN: Promise?

ANGEL: I promise.

UNBORN: Well, the galaxies are whirling. I guess it's almost time for me to start on my journey. Oh, that little speck of blue seems so far away.

ANGEL: But it isn't. We're really very close. Closer than anyone but God knows.

UNBORN: Good-by, then . . . good-by . . .

ANGEL: Oh, no . . . hello. It's always hello, beloved.

In the Shadows

The Ninth Woman
Eyelight
Tangled in a Line
Under Their Noses
Clumsy Beautiful

The Ninth Woman
(Midwife)

In some things you have no choice. You just have to do them whether you want to or not, regardless of whether you see much purpose in them. It isn't until afterward that you may wonder about them and about why things happened just that way to you.

Off in Rome, Caesar Augustus decided on a census, and we had to comply. So it began. It may have seemed a little thing to him, but to us, it was a major disruption. There was a lot of talk, resentment. But you couldn't do anything about it. Everybody had to go to the place of their ancestors to be counted. We went to Bethlehem, Amos and I and our children, because that's where his family was from. The thing I couldn't figure out was why we had to be counted. Some said it was for taxes. Since we had nothing anyway, such a long hard trip seemed doubly ridiculous to us. But we had to go, so we went. And little Deborah was sick all the way; burning hot she was. It is hard enough taking care of a family at home. Traveling, it's impossible. But you do what you have to do.

As it turned out, the morning we finally got to the place where the Roman legionnaires were asking people all the questions and writing down the answers on long scrolls, I was the ninth woman. I don't know why I remember that. The soldier asking questions called out for another to write down, "Amos of Godara, the fourteenth man on this day, with four male children, three female, and his wife, the ninth woman." And all the while, they were joking among themselves, paying little attention to us, really.

It was hard and bare, a number like that—so simple and matter-of-fact and distant, somehow. I remember shivering and I remember my feet hurting and Deborah being so hot . . . the ninth woman . . .

Afterward, when the man said that was all and we could go, there was no place we could stay. Those who could afford it stayed in the inn. Some had family in Bethlehem who could put them up. We less fortunate ones, well, we did the best we could. A man Amos met said some people were being allowed to stay out behind the inn in a cave where the animals were kept. So we went. It was out of the wind. I remember the wind that night, and I recall hoping Deborah wouldn't catch a worse cold. We found some water for her and we shared a little bread. It was a bit crowded, with all the people and animals.

Then . . . over in a corner of the place, this woman started to groan and make sharp cries like a wounded animal. I knew immediately what it was. I felt sorry for her. It wasn't much of a place for giving birth. But I knew I'd have to help, too, and that was irritating. I was so tired. Wasn't Deborah's being sick enough? And the other kids crying and being so restless? But, you do what you have to do.

The woman's eyes were wide, frightened. The pain of it seemed to surprise her. It often does the first time. Her husband didn't know what to do, except to keep reassuring her. Birth's too much for most men to understand. For most women, too, I suppose, but you have to take care of things first, then figure it out later if you can. Most men can't do without answers before they try anything.

It took a while. It wasn't an easy birth. It was good I was there to help. Knowing how it was, I could tell her about it, and that seemed to calm her. I told her to scream if she had to and bite her shawl—not her lip. And I reminded her that the pain was helping the baby get out. When he finally came, I cleaned him with straw, as you do a newborn animal. The father gave me an old blanket he'd gotten somewhere. I wrapped the baby and gave him to his mother. She was exhausted. And so was I, but I was glad I could help.

There's nothing like seeing what happens between a mother and a baby in that first few minutes. I've been there lots of times, helping in my little village of Godara. But never in a stable. Yet, the strange thing is, I felt it then, too, that special thing between a mother and a baby.

The woman looked up and asked me what my name was. I told her "Leah." And she said, "Leah, this is Jesus." I smiled. It was the first time anyone had called me by name since we left home. Not a number, a name. It felt . . . good. I touched her forehead, and Jesus' cheek, and held her hand for awhile, until she slept.

Deborah was still hot when I went back to my family. I lay down with her and held her very close. The children were all awake, but quiet in the dark. Just their eyes moved. They'd seen. It was like they were struggling with a secret and didn't know how to ask or tell it. And I didn't know how to tell them either.

Some nights, like that one, the wind whispers and it seems somehow like more than the wind. And children are quiet at the end of the day. Little things happen, and somehow they don't seem so little. But, it isn't until afterward that you may wonder about them and about why they happened just that way to you.

    "Leah, this is Jesus."

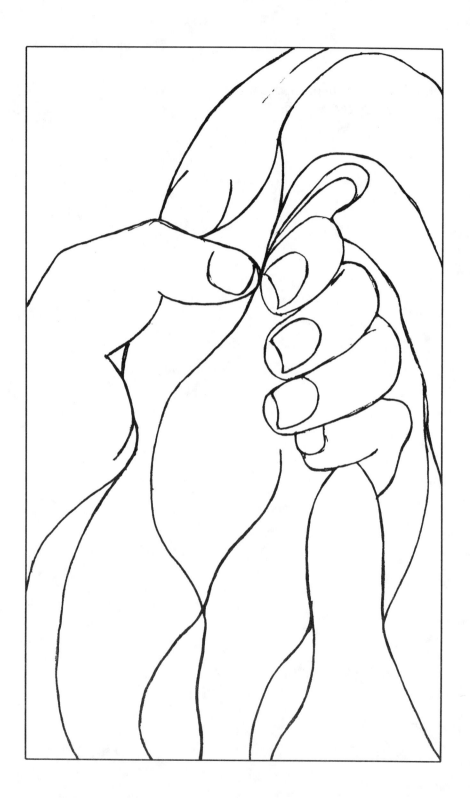

Eyelight

(Stable Hand)

Working all my life in a stable, I've seen lots of creatures born—sheep, oxen, donkeys. Most births are easy and natural enough. Some you have to help along. But, either way, you never get used to them. It's awesome to watch the struggle, to see the young one all tired and worn out afterward, and the mother, too. Then you can't help smiling, watching the mother washing her baby with her tongue. And then the little one working so hard and finally standing, all wobbly, and walking around all curious like, but staying close to its mother. No matter how many births you've seen, each one squeezes your heart, all right, and makes you think about things you usually don't think about, busy as you get doing your work and trying to keep your life together.

But there was one peculiar birth happened once, long ago, that I won't ever forget. There wasn't any room in the inn. I knew that, working there, but it wasn't any skin off my nose. The stable and the animals were my business. I kept out back and left the rest to the others except when they made me help. So when those families came along and asked me if they could spend the night in the stable, I said it was all right as long as they didn't get in the way of my work or bother none of the animals.

It was really crowded in the stable because of all the guests, their beasts adding to the ones we had. You never heard so much bawling and whimpering. All night I was mucking out the place the best I could, trying to find enough new hay, quieting down the more skittish animals.

So I'd almost forgotten about those people I'd said could stay there until a man came looking for me and said his wife was having a baby. He asked if I had anything to wrap the child in after it was born. Such an interruption was all I needed on a night like that one! I was about to tell the man to see to it himself as best he could, when a light from somewhere outside caught his face just so. I don't know exactly what that light was. The moon? Someone passing by with a torch? A shooting star maybe? All I know is that it was strange. Even now, I shiver to think of it. And the wind seemed to rise up just then, too, like a spooked colt wheeling and galloping off across the meadow.

Anyway, there was that man's face in the quick light, I don't know how long... a minute, a lifetime. But I don't ever remember seeing a man's face so sharp and clear before. The deep lines around his mouth. The play of the jaw muscles rippling the beard like a breeze caressing a grain field. And the beads of sweat over that upper lip where there is that little crease. (Jake, who works in the kitchen and is a little mad, says that crease is the print of God's finger which God lays on to seal your lip just before you're born, so you won't speak of the secrets of where you'd been or the worlds where you came from before you entered this one.)

But the man's eyes! His eyes were what stopped me. They were so deep. So tired, so sad, somehow. Yet, they were so strong— like they looked right through you; like they had looked right through almost everything and knew awful, wonderful secrets. Eyes that had the same kind of light as a rising sun etching out lonely peaks and shadowy valleys. That light . . . in his eyes . I remember those eyes. I guess the way to say it is that there was love in them, and . . . love always gives you pause . . . sort of takes your breath away. Does mine, anyhow!

The man said a woman from another family staying in the stable was helping his wife. They needed something to wrap the baby in, cold as the night was. So I got a blanket. Worn, it was worn, but clean because I'd washed it good after my dog, who used to sleep on it, died. My dog and his dying crossed my mind as I handed the blanket to the man and followed him to the corner where him and his wife had hunkered down. Strange how the cycles go: death and life being linked, one leading to the other so definite, so natural, but so mysterious all the same.

Anyway, I saw the birth. It wasn't easy, like a lot of them are. I don't know who fought the hardest against it, the mother or the baby. In any case, it did seem that neither of them were too sure they wanted it to happen. But nature paid them no mind. At last there was one final groan, followed by a sharp cry, and then a calm that was like that deep quiet moment just before or just after a storm. Even the animals seemed to sense something extraordinary was happening. They were absolutely still. I remember feeling that this birth was different, too, though I couldn't have told you exactly how.

So the woman who was helping wrapped the baby up in my blanket and handed him to his mother. The father's hands were huge and rough, and right then he put one hand on his wife's shoulder and the other on the baby's head. He was a tender man, I saw, for all of his being so big. The mother smiled, and she and her husband looked at each other for a long time. I don't know what their eyes were saying, but it was something powerful and personal and . . . secret I guess. I had to look away. Some things are between just two, and if you interfere, even by accident, you're where you don't belong. But I remember those eyes . . .

When I looked away from them, I looked to the baby. Now, here's the thing I can't explain. That child's eyes were just like that man's eyes, just like his father's eyes. I know it makes no sense to say it, but it's true all the same. That baby's eyes seemed so sad somehow, yet so strong, with that same rising-sun-kind-of-light in them, burning like they'd looked through everything and knew awful, wonderful secrets, too. There was the same kind of powerful love in those eyes and I saw it, believe me. Don't ask me more about it. That strange light that night, I never could figure out where it came from... or where the light in those eyes came from ... or what made the wind sound like it did, like more than the wind. Like the wings of night birds flying, but you can't see them—just hear them.

So I remember, and I wonder about more things than I can ever mention without being called mad. And maybe I am mad now. But you do your work, and take care of what you can, and keep your promises... and you wonder. Especially when, some nights, the light from somewhere outside your window casts beautiful, haunting shadow patterns on the ceiling. You remember and you wonder about the light and the shadows and about all you dare to know and yet know not. You remember because you can't forget them—things like birth and death and . . . love. Especially love. But even as you remember, you don't understand much. And yet you do remember eyes and light and those shadows and the very silence of them which seems to say, "Glory to God and on earth peace . . . peace . . . peace . . . *peace!*"

Tangled in a Line
(Court Priest)

Sometimes you have to draw lines, and sometimes you have to bend them or even ignore them. But most of the time, you have to walk them; walk a tight line. The trouble is knowing which to do, when.

When is the voice of conscience more critical than the voice of the court? You don't always know. It's hard to keep your balance. And surely, you know too, it's easier to compromise conscience than to challenge power.

So when Herod calls, you go! It was early evening when he called, the time I'm speaking of now. It had been a long day. The temple in Jerusalem is always a busy place, and priests have responsibilities . . . a thousand responsibilities . . . that often keep me awake at night: the wall of the temple needs repair; oil for the lamps is running low; revenue from sacrificial animals is off; there are services to be got through. And always there are political pressures to contend with—Rome on one hand, the Zealots on the other. Do you submit to powers or resist? And if you resist, how much, how far? And always the pressure, the pressure. When does one find time to think about such questions, to reflect, to study? I tell you, it's hard to keep your balance.

The days are always long, and this particular day had been one of the longest. We were meeting in the courtyard, the chief priests and the scribes, talking about how Rome's tax rulings were affecting temple properties, when the message came that Herod wanted us.

I remember feeling uneasy, as I usually do when summoned by powerful people. Rulers are not to be taken lightly. The nation must be preserved. Herod often wants the help, the blessing of the priests. He is a cunning man. He could shut the temple down! People would rebel, but . . . against Rome?? It seems too terrible to contemplate. People would be slaughtered. This way, we give a little, modify, adjust, to keep the peace. But it's hard to know when to draw a line and when to walk it. You know . . . you know, don't you? Conform? Resist? When? How? Why?

Herod summoned.

We went.

The palace was in a turmoil about something. You could feel it as soon as you walked through the gate. The guards were tense. There was a tightness in the air. The sun set fiery that evening, and the walls of the inner courtyard were blood red up high, running down darker into the deep shadows where we walked. I was seized with a sudden cramp in the gut. Perhaps I just needed to relieve myself. Sweat broke out. Was it just pressure? Or something else? How do you know?

It was too late to turn back. Or was it? Perhaps my foreboding was for nothing.

In the outer chambers were three richly dressed men. They were obviously foreigners. They were just sitting there, nodding to us and smiling as we passed into Herod's inner chambers. The calm of those three men was eerie and added to my apprehensions.

When the door closed behind us, the air inside was heavy, rank. Fear makes the body stink, and Herod's breath was foul when he wheezed his question, his voice as tight as a tent rope in a storm: "Where is the Christ to be born?"

The question was totally unexpected. We were stunned. No one thought to ask him why he wanted to know.

No, I ... I thought to ask ... Had the Messiah—the one we had waited for—had he come? What did those three richly dressed men have to do with this question? What would Herod do if the Messiah *had* been born?

I thought to ask those questions, but ... Herod was obviously in no mood to be crossed. So I didn't! To challenge power is dangerous. The torches burned so still in their brackets on the wall. The knuckles of the guards were white around their spears. It was quiet as only fear can make it quiet. The air was so close you could hardly breathe. Another cramp hit me like a wave on rocks. Cold sweat broke on my forehead, ran down my back.

Every one of us priests knew what Scripture said about the Messiah's birth. So the answer Herod wanted was supplied:

> "In Bethlehem of Judea: for so it is written by the prophet,
> 'And you, O Bethlehem, in the land of Judah, are by no
> means LEAST among the rulers of Judah, for from you
> shall come a ruler who will govern my people Israel.' " *

Whose voice had filled the room in answer to Herod? Was it mine? Had I blurted out those words or had I simply thought them? In any case, the words echoed ... a ruler ... a ruler ... a ruler ... Herod was a clever man. What else should be said to soften those echoing

---

*Matthew 2: 5b-6, RSV

words? Power *is* jealous. I said nothing else. We were . . . I was . . . just trying to keep my balance.

That's hard to do, isn't it . . . keep your balance, I mean. Later, Herod ordered all the male babies in Bethlehem killed. Power is jealous. You have to walk a tight line . . . My responsibilities often keep me awake at night . . . and the memories . . . and the cramps . . . the cramps . . .

Pressures, always pressures. Privilege on one hand . . . and . . . I sometimes forget *what,* on the other. I wish God would make it clearer when you have to draw the line.

You know, what the prophet Micah really wrote was this:

"O Bethlehem . . . who are LITTLE to be among the clans of Judah, from you shall come forth for me one who is to be a ruler . . ."**

I wonder why, so long after, it's put the other way to Herod in the story?: "By no means *least"* . . . *"Little* to be among the clans of Israel." There is a difference. One way suggests Bethlehem is much less than the other way, less and yet . . . maybe more.

O Bethlehem, so little, so little . . . but sometimes a little makes all the difference.

O friends, take note of little things. Little things . . . your prayers . . . lines . . . choices . . . Oh, yes . . .

***Micah 5:2, RSV*

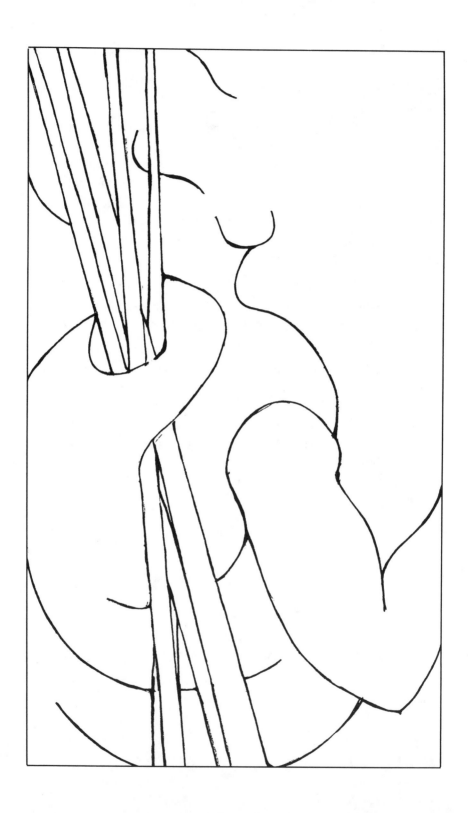

Under Their Noses
(Tent Bearer)

S tudying the stars is a good thing, I suppose. Yes, I'm sure it is! When I have time, I look at them and, well . . . they are awesome. I wonder what they are, and what keeps them up there, and what's behind them. But just looking at them doesn't give me any answers to those questions, though just asking the questions, the right questions, is a very important thing. For answers, though, maybe you have to study the stars a long time; I don't know.

The three men who hired me as a tent bearer for their journey studied them and spent much time discussing and pouring over ancient manuscripts trying to decipher their messages. And, as I said, I am sure that is a good thing, since their calculations and computations got us to our . . . destination.

But studying the stars can also be . . . well, misleading if you look at them long enough. And if you look at them exclusively, they become hypnotic. You lose touch with other important things. You just don't see those things, you miss them. And that is not good. Let me explain.

It was a hard trip over many days . . . or was it years . . . from where we started to where we ended. Now, a trip like that takes work. You have to pack food, prepare it every day, and repack it. You have to make fires, pitch and strike tents, feed the animals, rub them down, watch for pack sores . . . and a thousand other things. For a long trip three men like my employers need a dozen people to help.

And that's what I'm trying to get at. They hired us and then ignored us. I don't think they meant to, but they did. They just seemed to live in one world—the world of stars and philosophy—and we lived in another—the world of earth and people. When they needed us, they just assumed we'd be there: cooking, cleaning up, taking care of what, I guess, they thought were less important things. And I suppose it never occurred to them, either, to tell us what they were thinking or what the stars were doing. As I say, I don't think it was deliberate or malicious. They were just . . . well, absorbed in the stars, I guess. But the effect was the same.

Now, I admit feeling a little angry about their insensitivity. We could have used some extra help once in a while, especially during some of the storms. But it was like they didn't see. That's the thing. *They just didn't see what was under their noses.* They were so absorbed, so preoccupied with their own concerns and interests that they didn't see anything else. Now that I think of it, I realize the same thing happens to a lot of us . . . not just to people who study the stars, but to people who get stuck in their own little world and close out everything and everyone else.

Well, anyway, what I'm saying is that over that long journey, lots of things happened right under their noses that our three employers just missed, that's all. Abdul fell in love with Tamara, and it was . . . lovely, real, delightful. Elias, who stuttered and was so shy when we started, turned out to be a wonderful storyteller. Rhona played the lute for us so softly and beautifully, you would have thought it was an angel making that music. And when Raman, who took care of the camels, got sick, Ardis mixed herbs and mold and made a broth that broke his fever. Afterward, we all laughed and had a party with extra wine we fetched from the provisions, and cold meat and cheese. So many other things the star gazers missed as well: like the way the ground glistens when the soft early sun touches the dew; and the way a whole flock of swallows will wheel and dip and turn as one, as if on signal (but whose?); and the way your breath puffs out in little clouds in the chilly air; and the smell of the jasmine and the way rocks change their shapes, as if they are alive when the light and shadows play hide-and-seek around them; and . . . well, you understand my point.

So, we arrived, finally. It was a most curious spot. A stable. But our employers got out their gifts. Unlikely gifts they were for a baby—incense and spices and gold. Well, maybe the gold helped the family, but what I'm saying is that those gifts were picked and planned before we'd started, and those men were determined to follow their preconceived plans, no matter what.

I'm not sure they actually even *saw* the baby or, for that matter, the mother and father in that stable. Sounds strange, I know. I wasn't even supposed to have followed them in, though they didn't actually say not to. But I did follow, because I wanted to see what it was we'd come so far after. And it seemed to me that it was as if those three old wise men, if that's what to call them, didn't see that baby at all. I mean, they didn't smile, or chuck him a little under the chin, or kiss his head right there on the velvet-like spot on top, or any of that. It was as if, for them, that baby was really just as far off, as removed from the world as the stars they'd been studying. Funny thing . . . to have come all that way and still have missed it. At least, I think they missed it, because on the way back home, even though we took another route to throw Herod off, nothing changed between them and us. Nothing else changed either, really. I wonder how often that happens. Often, I suppose.

It's not that those three were wrong, necessarily, or that looking at the stars is wrong. But . . . well, that baby . . . his eyes were so wide open. And it seemed the whole time I was there, he was looking so hard, straining to see, like he'd never rest, 'til he had seen what there was to see. You've noticed babies doing that, I'm sure—heads up, bobbing around, hungry-eyed and seeking. Well, this one . . . even more so, more. It's like he was saying, "Stay grounded! There are mysteries at your finger tips. Don't miss anything. Don't miss anyone. Don't miss life!"

Clumsy Beautiful

(Servant Girl)

They're always yellin' at me in this place, especially on busy nights like that one. When it gets so busy as that, the owner of the inn is fit to be tied, and maybe he should be. I suppose he's scared that if somethin' ain't just right, it'll make some customer mad, and he'll lose a few denarii. So, the busier the place gets, the more he yells. He yells kind of quiet-like, you know, like a snake hissing. But there ain't no mistakin'; it's the same as a yell.

"Deborah," he'll yell. (That's my name and the prettiest thing about me, I've been told more than once—like I ought to have an ugly name.) "Deborah, get the wine goblets . . . sweep the floor . . . wipe up that vomit . . . get some wood . . ." and so on and on and on. Actually, he yells other things at me, too, but I won't repeat 'em. I try to ignore 'em and just do my job.

I'll tell you one thing they call me, though: Clumsy! I suppose I am, too, since I'm always droppin' cups, or spillin' wine, or trippin' over a door sill, or catchin' my dress and tearin' it on something. People laugh at me, 'specially the customers, and they say crude things to me. I don't understand why my body won't do what I want it to, but it won't. It is a . . . source of embarrassment.

I'm clumsy with words, too, if the truth be known. When anyone asks me somethin', and I have to answer, my throat gets tight and my mouth dries up, and I just go blank. Even with the other servants, I don't say much, though you mustn't get the wrong idea, thinkin' I'm shy and innocent or somethin' like that. I can tell a bawdy story good as the next one and hold my own in an argument, believe me. But pretty words seem as hard for me to get hold of as . . . the doves I try to catch sometimes out back. But it don't matter much, my bein' clumsy, since I'm just a servant and a woman. But that is what I wanted to tell you about, sort of. I wish I was better with words so's I could tell you about it so you'd understand . . . and maybe I could understand better myself. Anyway . . .

Oh, wait . . . another thing. I'm plain. I mean *real* plain! I think you ought to know that, though I ain't sure why, 'cept I think it's important for you to know me if you're goin' to understand what I'm tryin' to tell you. And the way a person feels about herself helps other people know her, don't it? I didn't say that too clear, but you get my meanin', don't you? Bein' plain is . . . well, a particular burden for a woman, I suppose. Oh, men pinch and pat and feel when they can. And they're always tryin' to get me to do things with them, sayin' things to me they don't mean. And sometimes I go with them just for the attention, even for a few minutes. And, to tell the truth, I like the feelin' of what we do together, if you know what I'm sayin'. But men don't mean nothin' *permanent* when it comes to me. Still, I'm not too much worse off than most women who get taken for wife. Just a little less secure, maybe.

Well, anyway, and truthfully, bein' a servant girl in an inn in a town like this ain't too glamorous. You get thinkin' you're sort of a beast of burden, a bearer of water and wood and dishes and nothin' much else. But to get to the point, that day, or that night I should say, I was feelin' 'specially that way . . . like a beast of burden. I'd been workin' all day and into the night. The town was runnin' over with strangers comin' in for the census takin'. The inn was so crowded and so noisy, you couldn't hear yourself think, and I had a terrible headache. I must have been up and down the stairs and out in the shed and back I don't know . . . a hundred, two hundred, five hundred times at least. Or so it seemed. I was trembly tired, in a fog almost. I'd fallen over people's feet a couple times, and once I just burst out cryin' and snuck into the pantry closet for a minute. It had been like that all week, really, and now it was halfway through the night and everythin' was still goin' strong.

"Deborah, you mangy goat, get some more wood." To tell the truth, I was glad to go outside. Maybe I could rest a minute, quiet-like. Goin' through the kitchen, I grabbed a crust of bread and slapped Nathan's hand away when he tried to get fresh. I pushed out into the night air and leaned for a second on the wall. "Bearer of wood and water and wine . . . and whatever else men want . . ."

Goin' across the yard, I munched the bread, gulpin' it down like I was starvin'. Then suddenly I tripped and fell in the mud. Right in the mud on my hunkies. Dropped the crust right in the mud, too, before I'd finished. I just laid there a minute, and then I started cryin', more from tiredness and frustration than hurt. Then I sat up and started laughin'; I don't know why. Maybe 'cause it kinda came to me, what I want to tell you about but don't know quite how.

What came to me was how still it was. The moon was hangin' up there so silver and soft-like, and the clouds over its face were touchin' it, gentle as I'd imagine a lover doin'. And the stars were like . . . like someone just lit them, like candles; and the darkness around each of them had crumpled and scattered like some really old lace or somethin' and was fallin' sort of like . . . like black snow all around me. And the cold and the mud and the light were all quiverin', like durin' your first kiss and you wonder what happens next. Funny how I'd never felt like that before or noticed how sweet bread tastes on your tongue before it goes down to calm your growlin' belly. Sittin' there, I felt like I'd waked life up, like it had been sort of sleepin' there unnoticed before.

And then I heard a baby cry somewhere. I've heard lots of babies cry before, but usually it's just annoyin', 'specially in the night when you're tryin' to sleep. But this time I wondered about it. So I followed the cryin' sound. And there in the stable, where old Naphtali works, was this family, this baby just born. I don't know what it was happened then. Maybe it was just noticin' that a newborn baby is ... well, what is the word for it? It is like ... like a miracle. I mean, there is this little thing and it's alive; all its parts are there; it's breathin' and movin' and makin' little sounds. How does that happen? I mean, how does that *happen?* I just stared. I don't have the words to tell you.

But I *can* tell you that right then, lookin' right into the heart of whatever it is . . . *right* then, and ever since, I felt beautiful. And proud, too, furious proud to be a human being, to be a woman, to be part of what produces a . . . a miracle like that or receives a miracle like that, even *is* a miracle like that, sort of. See, I am clumsy with words. But all the same, I just felt . . . well, strangely graceful, about me and about life and . . . even about the owner of the inn. Imagine bein' that close, that much a part of creation, of God. I do wish I could tell you better. Maybe you got your own words. I hope so. I hope you know how mysterious and beautiful God makes babies and people, even when they are plain like me and got mud on them. I hope you got the words for that . . . or the quietness.

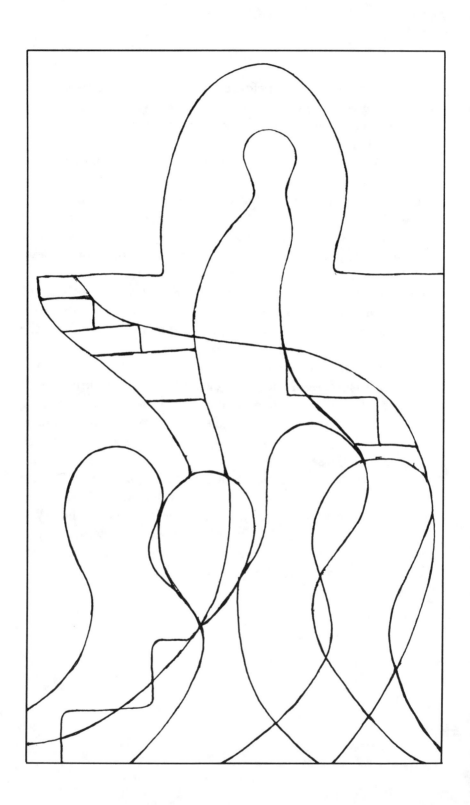

Steps in Time

PROLOGUE:

We're traveling, always traveling
the earth 'round the sun,
     the galaxy through space,
          the whole universe (they say) is moving outward;
               nothing is stationary.
All of us are travelers
     from place to place,
          from here to there,
               to somewhere!
All of us are travelers
     from time to time,
          from now to then,
               beginning to end!
Occasionally we pause along the way
     to rest, to eat and drink;
          to sleep, to talk, perhaps to think;
               to make love or to pray;
                    perchance attend some small thing
                         that might make sense of the distance come
                         or yet to go.

All of us are travelers
 from place to place,
  from time to time,
   from here to there,
    beginning to end,
and where we pause,
 or when,
  might be an Inn.
Call it whatever else you will,
I say it is an Inn—
 as then
  when a gathering of travelers came
   by Caesar's decree to be enrolled;
so now,
 do travelers come again
  by hope's decree to see unfold
   what happened then
    as happening still;
to hear,
 to overhear,
  perchance attend some small thing now
   that might make sense of us,
    of our beginning and our end.
Some word,
 a silence,
  a fragmented song,
   a signal fractionally clear,
    keeping time quite near,
as that night to this,
 and this to then,
  when all that was
   comes to is
    and moves to what will be.

A visit, then, to an Inn . . .
 Listen and see . . .

    *   *   *   *   *   *

WIFE: Oh, my feet!
               Things here won't ever be quite the same.
INNKEEPER: Haste, more wood.
               The fire is low and the guests complain.
WIFE: If not of the cold,
               they'll complain of the wine.
DAUGHTER: Or why their supper's
               not served on time.
WIFE: Or their beds are too hard,
               and the fruit is too soft.
DAUGHTER: Or there are too many folk
               for the space in the loft.
SON: I say, Caesar be damned!
               The enrollment's to blame.
               Just too many people!
               All they do is complain.
INNKEEPER: But trade at the Inn's never been this good.
               So, quickly, run out and fetch some more wood.
               Yet feed the fire carefully and as slow as you're
                   able.
               Our profits will soar if we keep our costs stable.
               You, run get the wine!
               You, run get the cake!
               Just think what we'll do with the money we'll
                   take.
               A killing! Praise Caesar!
               What a killing we'll make!
WIFE: A killing?
               What sort of talk is this?
DAUGHTER: A killing?
               What a curious twist!
SON: A killing?
               You'd dare to make real a wish?
INNKEEPER: Come, it's only a manner of speaking!
               I refer to the treasure we're seeking!
               Wealth—for a life of ease.
               Wealth—to do what we please.

Wealth—so our name will be known.
Wealth—to buy you children a home.
Wealth—for your pleasure, dear wife.
Wealth—to secure the good life.
Heaven knows, there's no law that I'm breaking.
You know, killing's just a manner of speaking!

WIFE: Pleasure?
My body's all bruised and sore.

DAUGHTER: Secure?
My bones ache to their core.

SON: Treasure?
Damn if I can do more.

INNKEEPER:
(to wife)
Run, run!
Our dream is here.
We mustn't miss it!

WIFE:
(leaving)
So the Inn is jammed,
but the dream's empty;
I've lost its point
along the way.

INNKEEPER:
(to son)
Hurry, hurry!
Success just waits for us to seize it!

SON:
(leaving)
Too many tasks, too little time.
My life's caught in a garroting bind.

INNKEEPER:
(to daughter)
Come, come!
Here's our chance.
We've got to take it!

DAUGHTER:
(leaving)
Get the wine, for the hundredth time!
I'm a broken heart 'neath a bitter rind.

INNKEEPER:
(alone)
Let's see.
I've made a list so I won't miss a thing.
You've got to be sharp to make a killing.
Now, fifty flasks of wine in each of twelve casks,
times sixty drinks each, at two coins, while it
    lasts,
makes . . . hmmm, I wonder what it was they
    were thinking.
They must know it's just a manner of speaking.

A killing? It's a phrase, nothing literal.
Nothing actual or serious or lethal.
I'm a good man and I've earned all I've got.
I'm shrewd and work hard, just as I've been
    taught.
I'm not for splitting philosophical hairs,
I keep my mind fastened on practical cares.
What's not useful's just a frivolous thing.
Add things up . . . and yes, make a killing.
I've made out this list, so I won't miss what
    counts.
I trace each transaction and watch profits mount.
Now, eight squares of cheese, twenty bushels of
    flour,
twelve racks of lamb, fifty guests served each
    hour . . .
Subtract just a bit for the cheap lutist I hired,
and food for his belly so his voice won't get
    tired . . .
(I'm told spirits improve as songs entertain;
I hope stomachs do, too, so the guests won't
    complain.)
How clever of me to arrange everything,
to make, as it were, such a marvelous killing.
Why does it seem so quiet here?
What's this cold? Has some danger come near?
There's nothing I see. This surely is queer.
The flesh on my neck is crawling with fear.
Maybe it's something I've forgotten or missed.
From the top I'll check once again with my list!
Why does my heart squeeze up like a fist?
Why does this awful trembling persist?

WIFE: *(returning)*	At the door, there's two need a room.
INNKEEPER:	Why this sudden feeling of gloom?
WIFE:	Husband! Do we have room for two, soon to be three?

INNKEEPER:	Riddles now? Wife, please speak plainly to me! Can't you see that I'm terribly busy?
WIFE:	The man's eyes plead of their desperate need. Surely we must pay them hospitable heed. If I'm any judge of her ungainly girth, his wife is ready to give immediate birth. Surely we don't have to send them away? Surely we can afford to let them stay!
INNKEEPER:	No room! Besides, they'd just make a fuss. No! They'd make too much trouble for us.
WIFE:	But where can they go? They have to rest.
INNKEEPER:	Not here! They'd surely upset our guests.
DAUGHTER: *(entering)*	There are eerie sounds in the wind tonight. Can't you hear how it hums and moans?
SON: *(entering)*	I've never seen the stars so bright. They touch with fire the trees and stones.
DAUGHTER:	Listen! The wind breathes the wildest melody.
SON:	Earth's awash in the strangest light. Come and see!
WIFE:	Those two at the door. What shall I say?
INNKEEPER:	Must I say it again? Send them away! You know that we're full, every corner and table!
WIFE:	But couldn't we find them a place in our stable?
SON:	Have you ever seen heaven's light shine so strong?
DAUGHTER:	Oh, the wind is heavy with curious song.
WIFE:	Now, what shall I tell those two at the door?
INNKEEPER:	All right! Please, I can't take any more. I've made a list to keep track of it all; now you're renting out an animal stall? Done! The deal: two denarii, but they're all on their own, and they've got to promise to leave us alone! For this is our chance to fulfill our dream; and to do that we have to follow our scheme! So let nothing whatever upset our plan

to take care of ourselves, get ahead while we can.
So, no more talk of the wind tonight.
And no more babble about the star light!
Let all your energies now attend
to the task that lies directly at hand.
Don't waste your time on any illusions.
Don't be diverted by idle intrusions.
Devote yourselves to the ways and means
that will surely make us kings and queens.
Now, pour the wine and cut the cake;
I've got my list, make no mistake.
I'm filled with glee when I contemplate
this amazing killing that we'll make.
Be busy!
Why does my heart squeeze tight like this?
And why does this cold sweat persist?
Go on. Don't dawdle! I insist.

(leaving)	I'll tell the musician he can play.
WIFE:	And I'll show those two where they can stay.
(leaving)	I'll charge them naught to ease my mind.
SON:	My life is in a throttling bind . . .
DAUGHTER:	I'm a broken heart 'neath a bitter rind . . .
	But there is a song in the wind tonight.
SON:	And the world is aglow in an awesome light.
	Something strange might be happening here.
DAUGHTER:	Something curious seems drawing near.
SON:	Just now, did you hear someone cry?
INNKEEPER:	Hurry, hurry! Precious time is passing by.
(calling)	
DAUGHTER:	I think I did hear someone cry.
INNKEEPER:	Run, run! We can make a killing if we try.
	But why do these tears fill up my eyes?
SON:	Yes, why? . . . why?
DAUGHTER:	Yes . . . why?

*   *   *   *   *   *

EPILOGUE

INNKEEPER: I never went.
When the last guests had gone to bed,
I cleaned the place.
After all, there's always something to do—
Put things away,
sweep and scrub,
measure and check,
count and plan;
your time is never your own!
But, I wonder, if it's not yours,
whose is it?
That's a night question . . .
Somewhere among the dirty dishes,
I asked myself,
if your time is not your own,
then *whose* is it?
Silence answered!
Quiet overrode the babble.
People slept.
They dreamed . . . of what?
Of beasts and shadowy things?
Of lovers, perhaps?
Of some resolution?
An easing of the torment? An ecstasy?
Dreams and labor—
the two are linked somehow,
as day and night are sides of time.
But whose time?
I labored and they dreamed.
Yet, somehow all were waiting
for some healing resolution,
for an ecstasy,
for some joy that is more than momentary;
waiting for love,
for whoever's time it is to be fulfilled.

WIFE: You say that now,
but last night I watched and waited a long time
    for you.
Not in our bed,
but there,
where the wind sang miracle into being.
When do dreams become the will to choose,
and love a time to be?

DAUGHTER: We sucked the wind
and gulped and hummed along
despite the smell.
Over the flanks of beasts caked with mud,
we watched for a lifetime.
There were whispers and, I swear,
strange carvings on the walls.
Unlikely place!
Still, where else do unlikely things happen?
Yet, you did not dare.

SON: I felt drawn by light that seemed to follow me.
I saw through night!
I tracked the cats and the quietness
and met strangers whose faces I knew not,
only their hearts—
the same as mine—
which leapt and knelt in the beat of a time
beyond killing.

INNKEEPER: I never went.
Spontaneity seemed an extravagance.
I had my lists.
What difference makes one baby, more or less?
There are bills to pay;
there is this rare chance, a killing to make—
perhaps of me.
I often wonder what is required of me . . .
and what do I require?
The two seem not a match.
Nor is there time for both.

Three hundred steps across the yard
from here to where they were.
I watched a time or two.
I hushed those men who yelled in the yard.
They left their job tending flocks;
I stayed at mine.
Ten steps from meat rack to cupboard,
four more to the door.
I watched there, for a time.
Ten steps to the cellar; six that way for the
    bread;
nine the other way for the wine.
Ten back to the kitchen; ten more to the dining
    hall.
Sweep the tables and set them.
What's left to be done; how much time before
    dawn?
However much it is,
it's just not your own.
There are claims and demands,
expectations, you know!
So much to be done, and whatever the time,
it's never your own.
Get mugs and plates for each place at each
    table—
crockery on wood sounds like thunder.
Three hundred steps from this hall to the
    stable—
I never went.

WIFE: Not three hundred steps . . .
only one—the first!
Time is choosing.
It becomes a matter of priority.
When there's not time for everything,
there is only choice time.

DAUGHTER: Not steps at all . . .
but a movement of the heart.

Time is keeping.
It becomes a matter of identity.
Who time gives you
when life's rhythm depends on your keeping
     time.

SON: Not steps
so much as the tracing of light.
Time is a given.
So lifetime becomes a question of dimensions.
What forever fills
is time open to the now of love.

INNKEEPER: I never went.
Three hundred steps,
or a thousand from here to there . . .
or only one—
just a heart beat or a lifetime never taken.
I never went.
But uncharted dreams still descended
which sweat as well as prayers attended.
Mysteries.
I watched . . . I heard . . .
A tongue I didn't know . . .
Movement in the shadows . . .
The singing of a bird . . .
A rustling.
It came to me:
transcendence is not asked of us;
just receptivity.
Or perhaps the kind of faithfulness
that is part curiosity.
And wonder enough . . .
or plain weary simpleness.
I heard what ears cannot truly hear.
In the wind, a cry.
I saw the chain of light traced across the sky
and fell in love
with old wrinkles and familiar voices

given life again somehow.
Everything dated from the now.
Lifetime become mine, undeserving.
In one moment born,
a promise made, and kept,
in the time of a life.
I never went.
One came,
and there was here,
then was now,
and that's the miracle even for me.
Not into the Inn where there was no room,
but into the shriveled womb of empty me
came the fullness of a time.
Christ is born!
Not too late, again . . . for you and me.
And there's the ecstasy!

Under, Back and Over

The Thwig Eater
Tickled from Behind
Trillia Minor

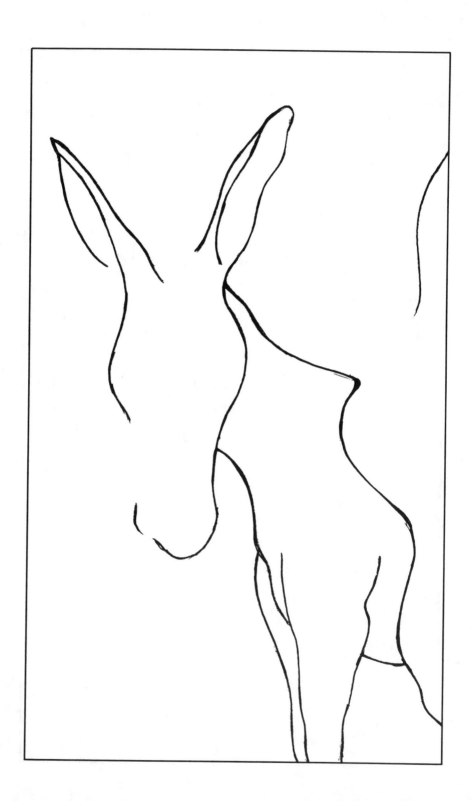

The Thwig Eater

(Musings of a Jackass)

Care for a thistle, anyone? These purple ones are my favorites. You're welcome to have one, really. They taste a little like what you two-legged ones call "basil." No? Well, all right. I find them a particular treat now that I am a very old jackass, so you won't mind if I have another, will you? That's why my name is Thwig, which is what we jackasses call this purple thistle. Thwig loves thwigs. Hee Haw!

Since I was there, I wish I could tell you more about the event of Jesus' birth, but everyone knows I am a dumb animal. But what everyone doesn't seem to know is that *all* of us really are dumb animals, whether we have two legs or four legs or many legs or no legs. We are more alike than it might seem. Of course, you two-legged ones know many things we four-legged ones don't. But maybe we know some things you don't, believe it or not. Which is why, just this once, I've been given the gift of speech so I can tell you what I can about the event. I wish it was more, but I wonder if anyone could really tell more.

Anyway, I know she was heavy as I carried her along that day, the woman whose name was Mary. I belonged to her neighbor, Elihu, and she and her husband had borrowed me for the trip. It was not something I wanted to do, carrying this swollen-taut woman and going so far from home with almost complete strangers. It was a job, just like hauling water jars and wool and wood and grain. She was heavy and withdrawn. And he was withdrawn, too, the one named Joseph. I sensed that they had been fighting before we started. You wouldn't imagine that sort of thing of them, would you, so gilded have you made them. But it was obvious that they didn't want to be taking this trip either. Every so often he would growl, "I just don't understand," and it wasn't clear whether he was referring to her being withdrawn, or the trip itself, or why he was with her at all, or exactly what. And when she'd answer, "Well, I don't understand either," nothing got any clearer except that they were having problems. I tell you that so you'll know everything about this event wasn't all "thwigs and clover."

The roads were clogged with people, and at certain places along the way there were Roman centurions urging everyone to move along faster. Occasionally there was a centurion riding some big handsome horse who would prance around and toss his mane and go out of his way to bump me off-stride, to prove how much better he was than I. He didn't have to do that . . . I already felt inferior. All my life I'd been called a stupid jackass, and I'd heard two-legged ones call others a jackass when they wanted to insult them. I knew I wasn't much.

I'm not sure I'm telling this very well at all. If what I'm saying seems about trivial and unimportant details, you'll just have to forgive me, because that's part of what I have to tell you.

As we moved along that day, Joseph kept tugging more and more urgently on the rope until the bit cut painfully into my mouth, and he kept muttering to himself things like "Damn Caesar,damn Rome, damn being too old for all this nonsense, damn Mary for getting pregnant." He wouldn't stop for anything. And the faster we went, the greater the distance grew between him and the woman on my back.

And the longer we went, the more she complained about being uncomfortable, about what were they going to do with this baby, about Joseph not earning enough to support them.

Meanwhile, all I could think about was how much further did we have to go, and would there be anything good to eat when we got there, and would there be a place to sleep out of the wind. What I am telling you is that all three of us got to be little more than beasts of burden. And we missed things.

We got to be little more than beasts because we seemed to feel we had no choice but to do what we were doing. But even I have choices. You two-legged ones do not say someone is stubborn as a jackass without reason! We four-legged ones have choices, too. We couldn't be called stubborn if we didn't! And if we have choices, how much *more* do you two-legged ones have them? Oh, not about everything, but about many things we all have choices. Choices are not just between alternatives, though that. The real secret of choices is deciding what those alternatives *mean*.

For a time that day we were simply beasts of burden; and the burdens we were beasts of were our resentments. I'm not sure how it happens, but when you clop along obsessed with a routine, it's easy to start feeling sorry for yourself. At least I do. The stones were biting sharply at my hooves, my mouth hurt, my back ached, and I resented having to do this job. I began to hate my owner for loaning me out. I thought about the thwigs I wanted and couldn't have. I thought about horses who weren't shaggy like me, who were more beautiful and talented, who had more to eat and better stables. Resentments grew like poisonous mushrooms in my dark, self-pitying mood.

Will you understand my braying tongue if I tell you I think the same thing was going on with Mary and Joseph? I tell you this so you will see, with some sight deeper than your eyes, that everyone connected with this birth was a dumb animal . . . but that is just what made this event so miraculous.

You miss things when you clop along with your head down, your nose to the ground; but the things you miss are still happening. That's part of what is so amazing. Mary's baby still moved and poked around inside her, in spite of her disbelieving and complaining. In spite of his cursing and fuming, Joseph led us on. And I carried this miracle on my back, even though I resented it.

But one thing we four-legged ones do that you two-legged ones forget is to keep in tune with all of our senses. As the day burned down, I heard a whir and looked up. The sky was the color of a thwig, and far off on the edge of the earth, two bright stars shone clear as a jenny's eyes when she sees her colt. The whir was the sound of children running at their before-sleep-games, though it sounded more like great wings in the air. Then the children laughed, and you could smell their delight. And in the long shadows, I saw a young couple holding each other so tenderly that I also felt caressed by something that felt like cool rain after a long trip in the desert. Then, for the first time, really, I felt Mary's fingers tightly wrapped through my mane. Suddenly I realized she'd been hanging on like that for the whole time, and the bravery of her hold began to sing in my blood.

So, part of what I have to tell you is that you miss things when you clop along, counting whatever you count when you get into a routine, or get obsessed with a job or a list or a goal. You miss . . . the little things, the precious things . . . the dumb animal things.

But there's another way you miss things. You miss things if you hold your nose up too high, if you insist that you're *not* a dumb animal. One time I met a lovely mare named Chigachig. (She said that was her name because that's the sound she made when she galloped.) Chigachig belonged to a wealthy man to whom Elihu sold wood. I met her when we took a load of wood to that house. Chigachig laughed at me for doing such lowly work and for looking so mangy. She said, on the other hand, she looked like Uguo Ogua (which is the name of the Great Mare who created all horses) because she was so strong and beautiful and smart, and because her coat was so shiny and golden. I asked her if she'd ever seen Uguo Ogua. She said she hadn't, but she was absolutely *sure* she looked like the Great Mare.

Well, since I had never seen Uguo Ogua either, I couldn't swear that Chigachig didn't look like the god. But I do know that Chigachig missed many things about herself, and me, and the world around her because her nose was so far in the air. For one thing, she missed that I loved her and wanted to be her friend. And she refused to try the thwig I offered her because it looked dirty.

But it is for another reason that I tell you about missing things if you hold your nose too high, a reason that is harder to get a hold of. It's just that when you start thinking of things in the abstract—too far off the ground—it is easy to get all twisted around. I mean, it's easy to get either envious or angry at Uguo Ogua if you only *think* about the Great Mare.

Let me try to tell you this way: Uguo means "Great Feeder"—the one who gives you thwigs and grain and cool water and green pastures. Ogua means "Great Rider"—the one who is always on your back, watching you, guiding you, perhaps digging at your ribs when you do things you're not supposed to. What I'm telling you is that it is easy to envy all the power you imagine Uguo Ogua having; and it's also easy to be angry at Uguo Ogua when things don't go right, when the thwigs are scarce and the loads are chafing. Then you miss the "dumb animal things" just as much as when you clop along with your head down.

All the same, I've heard the two-legged ones talking about their gods as we four-legged ones think about Uguo Ogua. The Romans say their gods are powerful and favor Romans over other people, and when two-legged people claim such knowledge, they are arrogant and cruel to others, as indeed the Romans are. They forget they are dumb animals, too, and strut around acting superior to everyone else.

But I've also heard Elihu and his friends talk about their God, Elohim, as though they had the same superior knowledge as the Romans claim. I've heard them say that when the Messiah—the colt of Elohim—comes, he will drive out the Romans and rule the world, and that the people who have obeyed his commands will share his reign. Yet underneath, this presumption makes them just like the

Romans. Such arrogance makes you two-legged ones miss things just like we four-legged ones do. Only we are not as good at such thinking as you are, perhaps because four legs are harder to get off the ground (and keep off the ground) than two legs. Still, we are more alike than it seems, we dumb animals, and we all miss things.

I tell you this because in the twilight, that day, I heard Mary whisper to Joseph, "You said we are to call the baby, 'Jesus'?" And he answered, "Yes. According to my dream, he will be the Messiah." I wondered, then, about such a dream, and if it could possibly be true that a Messiah could be born to such dumb animals as these two (forgive me for saying so). And if so, what might they miss about him? What were they *already* missing about him? What might all of us miss about such a Messiah? Will you understand my braying tongue if I suggest that what we'll miss is probably what we miss about ourselves? And this world? What we probably miss are the little things... precious things... dumb animal things... true things that we can choose because none of us dumb animals really have to be beasts of burden after all.

So, it was a strange night. The shadows felt heavy as water and seemed to part like the sea when the tiny ship of us moved through them. The darkness was laced with streaks of silver which shattered and braided together again as breezes flapped their wings, then perched again in the trees. The smell of supper smoke and apprehension mixed together, and there was a silence that was weighted with expectancy. It was a lonely time for the three of us. Something was happening. We'd all begun to sense it, and our silence changed from sullen to thoughtful.

Finally, Joseph found us a place in a stable, which was actually a cave with jagged openings on one wall through which the light and wind sniffed. It was a dirty, smelly place, full of other animals huddled out of the wind, animals caked with mud and dung. But it was shelter, and we entered it none too soon. There was a scream and it began.

Birth is an animal thing—sweaty, accompanied by screaming, bellowing, moaning, panting. It is full of blood and wonder. This one was no different, and the other four-legged ones and I watched, quiet, not spooked by the sights and sounds of it. This was something we understood. No, this was something we understood that we *didn't* understand, though we had seen it many times.

And there is always pain involved. It is not just physical pain, hard as that is. It is also the pain of being vulnerable, of birthing another life which will be vulnerable as well—a life separated from the womb where it was safe, protected; a life pushed out on its own; a life which, having begun, you know will one day end—and there is an aching kind of melancholy in that knowledge.

So there is pain; but without pain, life does not happen. Without pain, no one claims life. Do not ask me why. I just know it is so, know it through my skin and bones, nostrils and tongue. Without the pain, without the labor, the struggle, life simply doesn't belong to anyone; it doesn't have flesh and blood. Without struggle, life itself somehow becomes as unreal as Uguo Ogua, as a god who is only an idea off somewhere where no one or nothing can reach—nothing like pain or sweat or joy. Birth is an animal thing. It is a precious thing. It is an earthy thing. But that very mystery makes it a holy thing, a thing of God . . . blood and screams and all.

I wish I could say more, but I am a dumb animal. But I tell you that birth was a thing of God. That night the wind sang a miracle. That night the light seared the world and left scorch marks like a brand on it. The strange wisdom that peers from a newborn's eyes gazed out of that little, red, wrinkled one's eyes, out of that baby called Jesus. And I tell you, with this jackass tongue, that I knew then that God was with us: with all us jackasses; with all of us dumb animals of the earth; with all of us who clop along with our heads down or our noses up; with all the sullen, raging Joseph's, all the frightened, complaining Mary's of the world.

That far off One we give such names to as Caesar or Uguo Ogua or Elohim, or whatever your braying tongues name it, came to me. There it was, *there God is* —a little thing, an animal thing, vulnerable as I am, vulnerable as a mother's love is, vulnerable as any love must be or it isn't love. Who can envy such a God? Not Thwig!

We four-legged ones know we live by gifts—thwigs and a mouthful of grain once in awhile; a clear pool to suck water from, someone to scratch our ears sometimes because they care; a jenny or another jackass to run with or stand next to when a storm comes and jagged fire splits the sky and your courage shrivels—gifts to make your blood rush and sing a little. We know we live by gifts, and we are not so dumb as to refuse them. That birth was a gift! I received it gladly.

We dumb animals, four-legged and two-legged, are never such beasts of burden as to have no choice. And maybe that is what it comes down to—choosing, deciding for ourselves if it is true that God is with us in the little things, earthy things, dumb animal things. Will you understand this braying tongue if I tell you what I came to know that night? I realized that since God is not lost in the stars, we are not lost in the stars either.

That night I learned what power really is: it is the capacity to come close, to break through all the fences by which we try to make ourselves safe, even religious fences. The only way to do that breaking through is something as simple as sharing yourself. That's all . . . and that's everything. To share yourself is to be willing to make of yourself a jackass . . . or a child, or a friend, or a lover. That is what God did.

Love is the power to share yourself. And yet it is the only power we dumb animals really have. Will you hear this braying tongue if I tell you that this sharing is the only power that matters much? It is a risky power, though, sharing yourself. It is a power God gives us.

That's what I meant when I said I knew, looking at that wrinkled baby that night, that God is with us. God came to be with us, like a jenny in a storm. God came to help us to understand that since life is to belong to everyone, there will be joy in it. But since life does belong to everyone, it will also involve the pain of many births, the labor of many struggles, the struggles to share. So to claim life is not easy, no easier than carrying that heavy woman, Mary, a long way. But life is joyful, too. Yes, joyful like a backrub in the heart, like a thwig for the soul.

I think the power God gave us is the power to touch each other's hearts, to close the distance between us, to share ourselves even with our enemies just as God closed the gap between God and us in that bloody, wondrous birth in the light-haunted, wind-fluted stable. Something like that is what I was hinting at when I wondered what we would miss about the Messiah and about ourselves when the Messiah was born. For to miss that power of the Messiah is to miss something essential about ourselves. That power is the power to be vulnerable, which love is, or it simply isn't love. I know, because it was my daughter who carried Jesus into Jerusalem to die some thirty years after I carried him into Bethlehem to be born.

And the great mystery is that I carry him still. In some way I cannot understand, I am a bearer of his life simply because I live and am a dumb animal. So are you! And this once I have been given the gift of speech to tell you what I could of the story; I wish it could have been more.

Maybe, in these last moments given me to speak, I could simply say that, yes, I am a dumb animal; what is beyond me keeps me going: the splendid puzzlement I saw in the birth that night and the splendid puzzlement of me and of love.

What about you? For the rest of the story is yours to tell. For the wonder of the story is that the things we miss *do* keep happening. The child stirs once more, even in the disbelieving ones. God comes again, and the labor and the joy of it await. Oh, don't miss things this time . . . little things . . . precious things . . . dumb animal things. And oh, such holy things . . . such wondrous, holy things.

Are you sure you wouldn't care for a thwig?

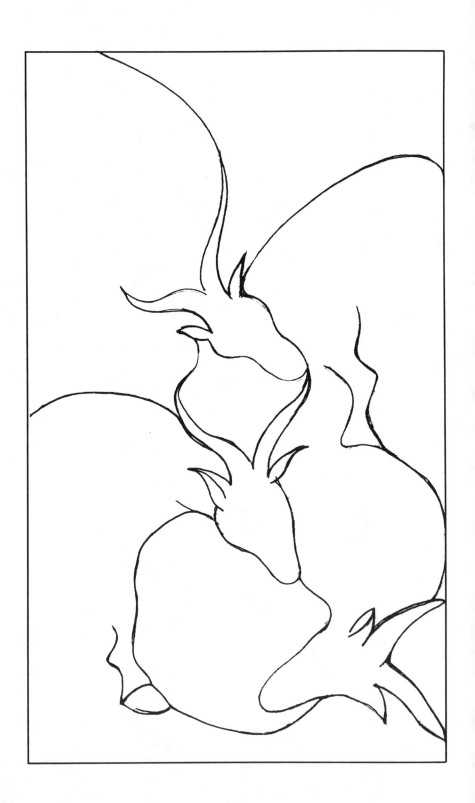

Tickled from Behind

(Dance of a Goat)

Hello? Hello! Jeez, I can't believe I can really talk like this, in your language. Okay, lean a little closer so we won't be overheard. The thing is, and you've got to hear this, someone is always out to get you, you know? You don't agree? Baa! Think about it. Most animals are forever trying to gain some advantage over other animals. They're trying to use you, get you to do something for them, put you down so they can climb up on you. Believe me, I know.

Now listen up! I only have this power to speak your language for a short time, and the catch is that if I tell you my *real* story, you probably aren't going to like it much, so you'll ridicule me... which is to say, you'll get me, one way or another. But I'm taking the risk, see, so try to pay attention. And if you feel stupid listening to a goat, think of how I feel trying to tell you anything in this idiotic language you speak.

Certainly one thing I want to tell you—maybe the main thing—is that someone is always out to get you. You think I'm exaggerating? Let me give you a little refresher course in my family history. You know the story of Abraham and Isaac—the one where Abraham is going to throttle his kid, Isaac, just to prove how faithful he is to God? By the way, there's a classic case of someone you'd never guess being out to get you—a father out to get his son.

Well, I haven't got time to get into all that except to remind you that having his old man about to get him like that scared Isaac so much he never got entirely over it, and he really never amounted to much. In fact, the only reason anyone remembers Isaac at all is because he had a couple of sons—Esau, who was such a dimwit that the other one, Jacob, took advantage of him and became famous as a result (which actually proves my point about people, even your brother, being out to get you). But I'm straying from my family history.

You remember the reason Abraham didn't sacrifice Isaac to prove his faithfulness? You got it! He found a goat for a substitute. So Abraham got the credit, Isaac got a reprieve, and the goat got the shaft. Now can you sense where I'm coming from?

And that's just the beginning! Whose entrails got read by Roman priests to foretell the future the gods had in mind for Rome? You got it! Goats! My uncles and aunts and cousins. And in the Jewish religion, when blood got scattered around the temple in certain rituals to make peace with God and then smeared on the priests to symbolize their consecration to God's service, whose blood was it? You got it! Goats'! You might say my ancestors were bloody religious. In fact, in the Jewish holy ritual of atonement, who did everyone transfer their sin onto and then take out into the wilderness and throw over a cliff so everyone got a fresh start with their God? Right again! A goat!

To tell you the truth, that's where the term "scapegoat" began.

You know about scapegoats, don't you? They don't even have to be goats anymore, can you believe it? As a matter of fact, everyone seems to *be* someone's scapegoat (and everyone seems to have a scapegoat). And scapegoats aren't just someone to blame anymore. Oh no! The field has expanded. Scapegoats are someone to use, to manipulate into doing something for you. And there you have the bare bones of what I mean when I say someone's always out to get you. You can flesh it out for yourself, now that you've got the point.

So I'm telling you, you've got to stay alert, keep a sharp eye out. If someone is out to get you, you have to dance around a little, be ready to duck and parry on a moment's notice. Goats, you may have noticed, kind of jump around a lot, but everyone has their own way of doing that. Come on . . . you know what I mean.

For instance, take a really simple thing. When someone greets you by saying, "How are you?," you don't just flat out say, "Hey, I'm the best thing around" (or something like that), if that's what you're feeling. Or you don't say, "At least I'm prettier and smarter than you," or "I'm really selfish and on the make," or "I'm sorry I ran into you, if you want to know the truth." You don't take chances and say things like that, even if it's true. No, you do a little shuffle and say, "I'm okay, fine. How are you?" So that way, everything stays nice and neutral, no hostages given or taken. But the trouble is, it escalates, doesn't it?

I mean, take when someone asks you what you think about some ticklish issue, or some animal you both know: you do the old "Watchit Waltz," don't you? You say, "Gee, I don't know. What do you think?" Or if someone starts tromping on somebody (maybe some scapegoats who aren't there—like nanny goats or black goats, or unruly goats or plain mangy goats), you stay quiet and don't say anything, even if you don't agree. Why? Because someone is always out to get you, and you have to protect your flanks, cover your rear. Right?

But oh, it is a wearisome business, isn't it? I was totally engrossed in it. That's part of my story, but now I have probably wasted too much time telling you about it . . . as though I knew so much. My arrogance is a cover, believe me. I really don't know very much. I just want you to like me, and I don't know how else to make you do that.

That's why I act like a know-it-all. You know what I mean, don't you?

I think what I've been trying to tell you is that goats have a bad name, and after a while that eats away at you inside. Why are we always chosen for sacrifice? What have we done to be singled out like that? I mean, it gets to you after a while, feeling so unimportant, such an outsider. I don't suppose any of you ever feel like that. I don't suppose any of you cover up like that. Maybe that's just a goat way of being.

Hey, let me get on with my story, the one I was given the power of your speech to tell you, the one about the birth. The birth happened at night, but earlier that day Quan and I left the herd and climbed high in the hills, as high as we could go. (My name is Zub, and Quan is my mate.) It makes me feel free and adventuresome to leave the herd and climb high like that. It makes me feel different, not just average like the other animals. When I look down on sheep in the pastures below, chewing their cud, huddled together like cowards, it is easier for me to accept that you two-legged ones think sheep are so cuddly and cute and much better than goats (who are considered to be poor peoples' cows). What's so good about sheep, after all? They are so insipid and unimaginative, so timid and easily frightened. I spit on them from my perch a thousand feet above them. Ah, but there it is again: I'm out to get sheep, to make them my scapegoats (if you'll allow me to apply that metaphor to sheep). Anyway, listen up!

It was cold up on the mountain, but it was as if you could see to the end of the world and beyond. There was snow on the high mountains across the valley. The grass tasted intoxicating. The air was so clear and sweet that only the tiny ripples on the little stream distinguished the air from that pure, fresh water. It was as if there were no other animals in the world except Quan and me. I said that to Quan and added, "Let's never go back. Let's live up here, free, on the summit of the world. No one would bother us. No one would take your milk anymore, or steal the kids to butcher or barter. No one would threaten us. No one could get us. We could live all to ourselves. We could do as we please. We'd be free, Quan."

Quan put her nuzzle against my neck and said, softly, "No, Zub. We wouldn't be free; we'd be a lie, a dream. The mountains are beautiful, and I love to be here. But there are other animals in the world, Zub. We can never live all to ourselves. Praca and Capra didn't make us that way. The gods go together, so their creatures go together." She rested her chin on my back. I felt troubled.

Praca and Capra are the goat gods. Two equal gods—Praca, the Billy god; Capra, the Nanny god. To be honest, I didn't have much truck with such nonsense, but Quan did. I knew I couldn't get anywhere arguing with her, but I tried anyway. "Look, Quan," I said, "let me tell you the way it is. In this world, which is the only one we have or know anything about, you have to look out for yourself, because no one else will."

She shook her head. I knew she'd start in about our owner, Naphtali, looking out for us and our friends among the other goats, so I cut her off first. "No matter what it looks like to you, animals are out to get each other, Quan. Believe me. You have to look out for yourself." She pulled away and looked at me.

"Why?" she asked simply.

I didn't really understand the reason, but I couldn't look at her just then. The answer to her question seemed so obvious, somehow; and yet, just because she'd asked, I knew it wasn't. She looked so beautiful and wise to me. The air smelled like it had been purged of everything dirty and ugly, even of death itself. I said, as much to myself as to her, "You have to look out for yourself in order to survive. I don't want to die, Quan."

And there it was, out in the open, up on that high mountain— my fear. I am afraid to die. Death is something I worry about a lot. I wonder when it's coming, how it's coming. I leap across chasms in the mountains as if I was fearless, but it's a cover. My knees shake every time I leap!

Somehow it was a relief that now Quan knew about my fear, but her response surprised me. Maybe she'd always known. She walked over and stood beside me for a long time, and then she said, "I think what you mean is that you don't want to lose your life, Zub."

Her words took me off guard. "Die... lose my life; it's the same thing, Quan," I blurted.

"Is it?" she asked.

"Look," I rushed on, "I'll tell you what life comes down to: sacrifice! Who sacrifices what for whom. And when the hay is finally in the barn, there are winners and there are losers. The winners last the longest because they sacrifice the least and get the most. Goats are a laughingstock because we're losers . . . consistently. That's why we have to look out for ourselves. I don't want to die. Let's stay up here, Quan."

For a long time she stood looking out over the valley, watching the shadows climb toward us until we were standing in the last sliver of light—a light that was so dazzling it seemed to come from nowhere. It was like a fire that burned only on that little outcropping of rock on which we stood. Then I heard the words, though I couldn't swear she spoke them: "It is your life you fear to lose, Zub, so you cannot stay here. If you do not make sacrifices for something, nothing is worth anything. Not even life. Especially not life." Suddenly I was dizzy. Was it the heights, the light, the words? Whatever, the world was spinning.

The next thing I remember, we were slowly picking our way down into the darkness. When I looked back to where we'd been, I saw that the splinter of light still burned, intense and clear. But somehow it seemed to have leapt from the rock to a place higher up in the sky where it appeared to be a radiant star. I attributed the delusion to my unaccustomed dizziness.

When we reached the valley, I wanted to stay out under the stars, but Quan needed to be milked, for she had come fresh even though the kid she'd birthed had not lived. If we went to the stable, Naphtali might milk her, though he might be busy working in the inn, especially since there were so many two-legged strangers about recently. In any case, we went to the stable, a cave out back of the inn. But we had scarcely entered and begun to get comfortable, when all the confusion began.

A man and a woman pushed their way in, stumbling over us in their rush to find a place to lay down. A jackass followed them. Strangely, I wasn't immediately angry or suspicious. I didn't resent this intrusion for some reason . . . maybe because their presence was so completely unexpected. Some things sneak up on you even when you keep a sharp eye out—like some jenny coming up from behind and tickling your ear and making you jump.

Anyway, it wasn't unusual for poor people to take refuge in a stable or even for a woman to get pregnant in a stable, if you'll forgive my goatish candor. But it *was* very unusual for a very pregnant woman to enter a stable; and this one was obviously about to give birth. She screamed and it began and we watched.

Will you believe me if I tell you that watching the birth had the same effect on me as standing high in the mountains that afternoon, where it seemed I could see past the end of the world? I kept hearing Quan's words: "If you do not make sacrifices for something, nothing is worth anything. Not even life. Especially not life."

Then it was over, the birth itself, I mean. Things happened quickly after that. The man cut and tied the cord, and the woman took the baby boy to her breast, under her shawl. Then Quan went over and nudged the man and somehow he understood. He found the milk bucket and milked Quan. Then he did a strange thing. He took the little baby and washed him off in some of Quan's milk, and Quan watched as if the baby were her's. After that, the man took a cup and gave the woman a sip or two of Quan's milk and drank the rest himself.

He went and got a rag somewhere, maybe from Naphtali, and wrapped up the baby. The woman kept whispering his name, "Jesus." I walked over and stood next to Quan and looked at the baby. I swear he looked back, and I tell you I had the powerful sense that that baby *wanted* to be there. I mean right there, in that cold, dark, smelly place, which in that instant did seem somewhere past the end of the world and yet close to the beginning of another one. I think he wanted to be right there with us . . . us goats, if you please.

Now you may think I'm being a know-it-all again—doing a clever cover up and making myself more important than I am. But I swear, this is the straight scoop. All I can say is that right then, I didn't feel like an outcast. I felt like I belonged. I felt connected to every animal of the earth. Still do, which is really strange.

I looked at Quan, and she actually winked at me. I knew she was thinking of what she'd told me up on the mountain: "The gods go together, so their creatures go together." All of a sudden it occurred to me that if the gods go together, then there's really only one God—Praca and Capra, male and female, goat and sheep, two-legged and four-legged, everything, is all one. But if the gods go together, why are we always trying to pull them, and each other, and ourselves apart?

The funny thing is that all this stuff about the gods felt different than it did up on the mountain, where it seemed like nonsense. Somehow, there in the stable, it felt right. It felt possible in that cold, dark place, looking at that Billy-goat-of-a-kid, because he *did* seem like a goat—the way he was making noises, kicking his legs so furiously, butting his head against his mother's breast and waving his little hooves around.

So I started to laugh. Can you believe that? I scarcely could believe it myself! But sometimes laughter is part of what a baa is, and when you hear a goat's baa, you at least smile, don't you? Anyway, I burst out laughing, belly baaing, and Quan joined in. Then that jackass brayed, and a dog howled, and a cat meowed, and, I'll tell you, it sounded like music. The laughter sniffed back at the wind and light that lurked around the openings of the stable. Then it broke out and rolled out over the valley, gaining volume as it washed down over the plains and trickled into every craig and cranny.

I laughed because the situation struck me funny! Here I was, always on the lookout because someone is always out to get you, and lo and behold, whoever it was who was out to get me had gotten me that night, right between the horns. Out on the mountain I'd seen and heard such awesome things: wind like the music of a thousand harps, scenes and colors beyond description, formations of clouds that looked like herds of strange animals stampeding in from beyond the stars, sunlight making rocks glisten like great mounds of wheat, awesome storms and booming thunder splitting the gaps. And yet, what I felt on the mountain was only great longing with a kind of deep sadness about it all.

Then some little things like this baby and this peasant mother and father groping into this forsaken, dung-drenched stable, snagged my attention and caught my heart off guard and spoke of . . . well, of God, or whatever that mystery is that every species of creature I've ever heard about gives a god's name to. That little, unlikely thing—that newborn miracle—whispered to me of God, I swear it though I can't explain it, and made my heart leap around like a billy-in-love. Yet it caused there to be a silence inside me that was wondrous as the stillness on a mountain summit in the moonlight. I mean, I couldn't help laughing. It was like someone snuck up and tickled me from behind.

Now listen up! When something like that happens, the things you thought were so terribly important begin not to matter so much—things like climbing so high and being safe and spitting on lowly goats. I mean, I started asking myself what was so important that it could account for my wanting so much to survive. So that's when I began thinking of Quan, and my goat friends, and those dumb sheep, and even Naphtali. I began thinking that what's important is laughter and what it's made of . . . like delight and . . . well, gratitude, and hope, and love. What's important is that mysterious link between me and Quan, and between . . . well, as she said, there are other animals in the world and you really can't love all to yourself. What's important is a nuzzle against your neck and trying not to let anyone make you a scapegoat, or make anyone else one either.

You see, I realized that night that it cost this newborn kid something to be there, in that dark, cold stable with us goats and jackasses and two-legged ones and all the others. It occurred to me it always costs a kid something to be here in this world. What was funny, joyously funny, was that, judging from his cock-lipped smile, this Jesus must have decided we were worth it for him to make a sacrifice like that—to *be* with us. I wonder if other kids do?

I looked at that kid, lying there, eyes wide open, gazing right at me. And I began to feel he was asking for some sort of sacrifice from me. And then it dawned on me. He just was asking me to be a goat and be glad of it. He was asking me to accept the sacrifices which being a goat involved. Nothing more, nothing less.

Suddenly, your language is getting harder for me to speak clearly. But those words I'd heard from Quan are right: "If you don't make sacrifices for something, nothing is worth anything. Especially life." But you get lost if you think sacrifice is always something enormous, a sacrifice everyone notices. Maybe a sacrifice involves small stuff, but crucial: like of time, of attention, of ambition, maybe; or of grudges and grievances, or making scapegoats of other animals—things you do that kill life. Maybe it's just risking being really free and daring new things, whether they make you popular or not. Perhaps then you're not so afraid of dying, because then you're not losing your life, you know. Do you follow me as I follow Quan in this?

So I laughed. I laughed because of joy, because love is possible . . . if you sacrifice for it. I laughed because . . . that stable was so full of life, and . . . I felt sure I would not lose my life.

So part of my story is about the power of laughter, and freedom has something to do with that power. I remember the priests making their sacrifices and looking like they'd just eaten a green persimmon. Do all two-legged animals think holiness and humorlessness go together? Believe me, they don't . . . and that's not just an arrogant goat talking! This is one goat who laughs at himself, and that laughter is something of what freedom is.

Persimmon priests! Maybe they don't laugh because the only sacrifices they make are of someone else or something else other than themselves.

But listen up, for my time for speech slips away. Laughter is a holy thing. Laughter is as sacred as music and silence and solemnity, maybe more sacred. Laughter is like a prayer, like a great hurrah, like a bridge over which creatures tiptoe to meet each other. Laughter is like mercy; it heals. When you can laugh at yourself, you are free. Listen to me . . . baa, baa. Quickly, the power of speech slips away. Baaaa baaaa.

Listen, that night—that improbable, cold, smelly, altogether wondrous night—I went to that kid, that Jesus, and I knelt down by him. There was a fleck of blood on his cheek and a bubble on his lips like kids get, and that crazy smile. And in his eyes was a star, I swear—a dazzle of light like the one on the high mountain that shadowy late afternoon. What light was it? It was like no light I'd ever seen, and yet it was like every light I'd ever seen. It was like all the stars in all the skies that ever were, gathered in one place and then, in a blink, scattered wide again, forever.

As I gazed at that light, I heard a chuckle, a chuckle I'll never forget the sound of . . . baa . . . baa . . . Oh quickly now, I'm losing my speech! Life was on his face, such amazing life; life I knew he'd never lose (even though you could imagine how people would scapegoat over and over anyone who was that full of life).

Oh God, my heart was full. So I did a funny thing, a spontaneous thing. I wanted to give him something, so I laid down and put my whiskers on his little feet to keep them warm. It must have tickled, because his chuckle turned to laughter. And Quan laid down beside me and put her head on that tired father's lap to keep him warm. So we slept a little. But every once in awhile, the baby would laugh. And once he lurched forward and touched my head, here, between the horns; and to this day my heart burns from the power of it.

Baa ... power of speech is fading fast now ... baahaha ... and I want to tell you ... baahaha ... again that someone is always out to get you, so stay alert ... keep a sharp eye out ... baahaa ... because that is what life is about, that life you don't want to lose, and won't, oh don't ... baahaha ... so listen deeply beneath all words, beneath ... baahaha ... beneath the noise on the streets, beneath the silence, under the silence, and ... baahaha ... you will hear the laughter, like a beating heart, like the gurgle of a baby, like ... baahaha ... the bleating of a goat ... baahaa ... like the love of God ... baahaa ... ha ha ... ha ha ... And, oh, join the laughter. Laugh at yourself, laugh in joy. For not to laugh may be to miss the one who is being born among us even now. Keep a sharp eye out. Listen. Someone's out to get you. Praise be, praise baahaha ... ha ha ... haha ....

Trillia Minor

(Song of a Swallow)

H ave you seen me fly? Wingless ones, such as you, have been known to envy our power of physical flight, and there are stories about the disasters such envy has produced. But you do fly, really, and you certainly do sing, as we birds do. Often I hear you sing, and your singing draws me to you, as a sister or brother, and I fly closer to you, just as that night I flew into the stable when I heard the baby crying, which is a way of singing, too, you know. Oh, what a night it was. Do you want to hear of it? But, of course, you do. How silly of me to ask. Come to think of it, that's how it is that I can speak like this, so I can tell you.

Well, I was the only one who left the flock as we pitched and wheeled through the sky that night. How can I tell you what it is to fly? But you know really, in your dreams and in those vast spaces that stretch within you as far as the heavens stretch without. If only you would explore more of that way of flying, then you truly would know the secret and the truth of the feeling that there's really nothing between you and forever.

That night, the flock of us flew on and on, as if there was no time; as if the glorious twilight simply forgot how to become night and lingered on, touching the edge of day like a lover unable to leave his beloved. I cannot explain how the light shimmered all around us, yet if you looked for its source, anywhere, all your eye caught was darkness. Was it a strange tilt of the moon or some peculiar fall of starlight? Or, more wondrous still, was it perhaps the darkness showing its other side? I am much too simple minded to know.

All I can tell you is that there was a glow that night so eerie and awesome that it stirred in us an irresistible urge to fling ourselves toward it, though, in truth, it seemed to penetrate us as well, until we glistened in the sky like drops of water flung into the air where they catch a glimmer of sunlight. Ah, but you have known such nights, though you may have forgotten or disbelieved them.

And more, that night was wrapped in wondrous sound. It was like a thousand brooks tumbling over rocks in the mountains, like a choir of nightingales scaling the vault of heaven, like a squadron of eagles screaming triumphantly, like the tinkling bells of the lead sheep of every flock on earth . . . all at once, everywhere. Yet, when you turned your ear to catch it, there was only stillness and nothing moved. Was it the wind, or the rustle of our wings, or the beating of our hearts? Or, more wondrous still, was it perhaps the silence whispering its other side? I am too simple minded to know.

All I can tell you is that the sound that night stirred an irresistible urge in us to lift our voices and hurl them to join (or perhaps only to echo) that radiant spill of music. Oh, such a night of silver and song it was; and, in truth, you could not tell the silver and the song apart. What a night it was—a night such as you have known, surely, though you may have forgotten or disbelieved it.

But then, soaring in that forever sky, I heard the baby's cry. Do you doubt it, that I could hear such a pitiful cry while flying so high? Oh, doubt it not! You know us birds as creatures who can fly, oh yes, swiftly and gracefully. And you know that we can sing, for sometimes you even listen. But you must not forget that our eyes and ears are amazingly keen. We can hear such small, strange things, and see them, too. So, yes, I heard the baby cry, there in a crude stable a thousand feet below. I left the flock and flew to it, as if that stable were the only place in heaven or earth that it mattered for me to be. That is where my story begins, this story which for a time—a very short time, I am told—has turned my song to words you can hear as your own.

I heard the cry, and I entered the stable silently, gliding to a rafter braced to hold the crumbling roof in place. I perched and watched. Everything was old there. The stable itself was as ancient as creation—a cave in which Adam and Eve might have stayed—now decrepit with the feel of a hundred generations of forgotten families who might have made their home there in times past. The animals present were heavy with the aura of age, or agelessness, which animals easily acquire. The birth itself was as old as time, as were the primitive, ritual, fretful tenderings of the parents. Everything there was old.

Yet everything was new, too, and that really was the strongest and clearest sense. Everything was new as life, as new as something beginning and so triggering other beginnings, especially for the man and woman who were half lost in their contemplations, occasionally looking at each other shyly, wanting to touch with words but managing only with fingers. Slowly I realized that everything about that night, everything about the silver and song of it, spun around this scene. I watched.

Most of all I watched the baby. I could scarcely believe it, but he watched back. I have never known one so freshly hatched who could watch so intently, for such a prolonged time, but this one did. Perhaps it was that my quick movements caught his attention, or that I was perched directly in his line of sight. But I tell you he was all eyes. All eyes! He seemed never to take his eyes off me. I swear it. He was the only one who saw me that night in that place. The others didn't notice, or they didn't look. But he did. And so my story grows in that.

He saw me! Do you have any idea how amazing that was to someone such as me? Do you know how cheaply birds are valued in this world, what little consequence we're given, how we are taken for granted? Well . . . perhaps you do! Perhaps you do, you who sing, too, and want so to fly.

Yet, he was all ears, too. Can that be? I know not, simple minded as I am. I only know that when I sang, he heard me. But did I really sing? Was my song soft or actually silent? Was the sound of my song like the sound of the night that no one of the flock could locate? Was it the other side of silence whispering through me? I know not. I only know he heard my song, the one in my heart; the one I wanted to sing and somehow must have. For he heard me!

So I will try now to tell you the strange secret in the heart of my story. I thought I came to that place to *see* something, to see who had cried. But no! I found I came there, to that baby, to *be seen*! I did not know that, nor would I have said it until it happened.

Oh, my featherless friends, I ask you, do you really think we go anywhere, any of us, just to search for something, just to see something that might be for us the key to understanding things or to find something that will satisfy our ravenous hearts? Do you really think that is why any of us move so fast, try so hard, scratch so frantically, work so hard? Oh, maybe we do think that. And maybe it is partly true that we do all that to search for something, to try to see some secret that will make heaven and earth known to us.

But something in us knows that what we really want is to be seen. Not merely noticed, not taken as an impression and put into a cage, a category, but to be seen, *truly seen,* to be delivered into life by a gaze, gasping like a baby; startled into awareness by a look so penetrating, so steady, so powerful, that we sense forever after that we are known and will always be remembered.

So it was that night for me, Trillia the swallow. He saw me! He saw Trillia! The only Trillia that ever was. And then there was in me a flood of fire and song, a thrill that teared my eyes, shivered my feathers. It was as though that was why he was born. It was to see me; and to see them, everyone else in that stable, every other creature on the earth, to see us so we would forever know we are seen. Do you understand at all? Oh, please, you must. You do, surely you do?

Somewhere in those vast spaces that stretch within you as far as the heavens stretch without, you do understand what I am telling you. Don't you? Don't you?

Oh, I am such a bird brain. All I know is that he saw me that night, and he was the only one who did. No! No, that is not right. Part of the secret of that night was that *I saw me*. Maybe for the first time, I saw me . . . because he saw me. And so I sang that night, as for the first time. Oh, I don't know how to say it. All I know is that I have never forgotten his gaze. It looks back at me wherever I look; it resides in the eyes of every bird I see, every song I hear; it squints at me whenever the light shines, whenever a baby cries. His eyes . . . all eyes . . . and I am seen. Oh, I rejoice in that and hurl myself toward heaven and sing, sing, sing.

My song would be better than words, I know. I wish I could sing for you now. Still, I must try to tell my story, else why were words given to me? Let me try to tell it another way. You think singing is natural to birds, don't you? Well, in some ways it is, yes. We sing just as naturally as you rejoice—no more, no less. For us, it is the very blueness of the sky, the warm whirl of the sun, the abundance of bugs and seeds, sweet dew in the morning. These lift us and set us singing, these and dry nests and a mate and little ones so fierce in their passion to fly. Singing is natural to birds, just as it is to you featherless ones.

But we seem to lose most easily what is most natural. It isn't that we don't do those natural things; it's that we lose what they mean. We lose the life in them. Oh dear, I'm not telling you my story much better this way, am I? I think it's coming unraveled.

What I'm trying to tell you is that we lose our natural capacity to wonder and to rejoice. We get jaded. We fear being embarrassed. So we pretend we've seen it all. But underneath, we keep looking for something—something that will be the key to understanding things, something that will satisfy our ravenous hearts. Such a tragic split.

Because of the split, our wonder molts into envy—envy of others who seem to have what we don't, who seem to get what we don't, who seem to be what we aren't. I have watched many things as I've soared, and I have noticed that it is hard for creatures to be glad for the gifts and good fortune of others. It seems especially hard for you featherless ones. You make criticism an art, and seldom do you praise anyone, even your God, without adding a criticism. So you pluck the feathers off wonder and nest in envy.

And you don't sing anymore. Oh, you make sounds, but you don't sing with your heart in it. And there is no song if your heart's not in it; there are only notes, only techniques, only imitation, only pretense.

There is a saying among us swallows which is, "You can't sing if you don't hear the song." That's why I tell you that I sang, maybe for the first time, that night. I sang because I *heard* the song, and the song was simply, "You are seen. Always and everywhere and forever." We are not lost. We do not live and leave no trace. That's my story. We can sing because that's the song.

I know, I know! Swallows don't sing. That's what you say, isn't it, you and your bird books? And you are right. Mostly you are right. Oh, sometimes we sing, some of us. But mostly we twitter. You recognize twitter. It is our common, universal language, isn't it? Twitter is what comes out when you sing and think the song is yours, the voice is yours, that *you* are what the song is about. Twitter is what comes out when you sing for your supper, you know, sing for gain, for deals and alliances, for advancement.

I should tell you the wisemen came that night to kneel before the baby, but powerful people often go through those motions just to keep fences mended, to establish useful relations. Powerful people don't understand that the miracle of a child is more wondrous and weighty than all the splendor of market and state. So they twitter. Yet others in the flock don't often dare to call it twitter because they are so afraid of the powerful ones and what they might do to them. So, obsequiously, they call it a song, and this is twitter, too, the worst kind of twitter, really.

In any case, you have been in a flock of featherless ones, haven't you, and heard the twitter? You have heard, in every gathering of the flock, the way people begin to talk about themselves, twitter to impress you with what they know, or who they know, or what they've done.

But have you heard under that twitter the great need, the deep longing of those creatures for affirmation, for love? Do you hear that longing under your own twitter? Well, that is why we all twitter. We want to be important to something, to someone. We want to leave a trace to prove that we are real, that we matter, that somehow we won't be forgotten, that we are not of cheap value or no consequence. Even a bird, falling to the ground, wants to know it is not forgotten, that it is loved somehow. Oh, how much we all want, how much we all need to be seen!

That's what I suddenly recognized that night when he saw me. And now, I tell you, he sees you. Do not ask me how I know, only do not doubt what I tell you.

Listen! That night, much later, I slipped out of the stable and flew again. I simply could not contain it—the power, the incredible love of his gaze. I rode it up, up, higher, higher, so high, so high. I rode that gaze as high as eyes can see, as high as you yourself must ride your dreams sometimes, though you may forget or disbelieve it later. I rode it to the stars and beyond, to Pleides and the polestar.

And then, I looked down; and what I saw is the rest of the secret wrapped in the heart of my story. I saw things differently. You can imagine that, can't you? You can imagine how if you stepped over here or over there, or if you flew way up or plunged way down, you could look at the same things you'd seen before and see them differently. You can imagine how maybe you could even look at time— look at the past or perhaps the future—and see it differently, too.

Well, I looked down that night on the earth, and it was lovely beyond all telling of it. My little tongue flaps helplessly now. But then the shadows crashed like symbols, the clouds hummed strange litanies, and the earth . . . the earth rang like a bell. Everything laid out before me, and I was suspended (like a little feather, a tiny bit of grit) somewhere between now and evermore. But what I saw was not so much how small I was, but how inseparably *connected* I was to it all, to everything, to the brightest stars in the heavens, to the dullest, tiniest stones on earth.

And I tell you, my featherless friends, you are a part of it, too, part of that enormous, splendid whirl of life and wonder; only a part—a small, small part—but a part still and all, inseparably connected. Sometimes you let yourselves become so earthbound, so timid and hesitant about those vast spaces within you and without . . .

and about knowing how to fly . . . that you forget, or disbelieve, that you are part—part of a holy thing, part of the light, part of the song. You forget you have wings that bear you up; that you, too, ride the gaze of love that stitches you to everything forever.

Oh please, hear the song. *You are seen.* Rejoice! Rejoice with those who rejoice, with those who have gifts you may not have, who can do what you cannot. For rejoicing with them, and for them, and in them is the way to be blessed by them. Rejoicing is the way to be part of it all, of everything, part of . . . life, of love that goes on, and on, and on—like flying when twilight forgets how to become night. It is a way of sensing God is with you in everything, even as the light that night may have been the other side of darkness, even as the sound that night may have whispered of the other side of silence. The baby is all eyes. We are seen! Even this little bird is seen, and every little bird.

Oh, I flew with the angels that night. So do not doubt it, though I cannot tell you now of their appearance—what their raiment was or the number of their wings. But do not doubt that I flew with angels that night, for you have heard them, too, and flown with them yourselves, though you may have forgotten or disbelieved it. I flew with the angels that night, but I cannot tell you of it in words. I can only sing it, for some things can only be sung.

But here's the joke, the enchanting joke of it. I wouldn't sing if I weren't a bird brain. With a brain as big as yours, my featherless friends, it is a terrible temptation to think too much. To sing, you have to let yourself become a little crazy. Or a little childlike or a little bird-like. You have to let wonder have its way with you. And singing is what this celebration of Jesus' birth is about.

Oh, quickly now. Sing! Sing! You can sing because you have heard . . . my story. You are seen! So sing! For the most curious mystery of all is that, incredible and glorious as the song is, it isn't the song but the *singing* that matters most! Oh, please do not think I have just contradicted everything I've told you up to now! Please!

You see, the mystery is that the song has many parts. Many, many parts. There are parts for swallows and nightingales, for angels and four-legged ones, and for featherless ones, too, all kinds of featherless ones. The wonder of the song isn't that there is only one song for every creature, and every creature must sing that one song. No, the wonder is that all the different singing of all the different creatures makes up one song. Do you understand my story at all?

Oh, do not doubt it. It is the singing that matters. What matters is to be a little part of it, for the music is less, so much less, without your singing, without each of us singing. The song is just loaned to you for life, loaned to each of us—a loan this season reminds us of and renews in us. Our part is to sing the song back with whatever ruffles and flourishes we add of our own.

So be done with twittering. Sing from your heart. Dare to rejoice. Yes, dare. For it does take courage to sing from the heart—courage and craziness, which may be the same thing, at last. Cowards do not take chances. They do not rejoice. Oh, dare to sing. Dare to sing.

For I tell you, the One whose birth you celebrate this Christmastide was all eyes, is all eyes. He is there, all eyes, and you can never forget, because that gaze is a presence that abides with you always.

> God is there, looking back at you wherever you look—
>   in the eye of every bird,
>   every crazy bird you see;
>   there in every song you hear;
>   squinting at you whenever the wind blows,
>   wherever the light shines,
>   whenever a baby cries or a child laughs,
>   or a woman dances or a man sweats;
>   looking at you, claiming your love
>   wherever a family hungers
>   or a creature is oppressed or brutalized
>   by war or threat of war,
>   by poverty or prejudice,
>   by injustice;
>   looking at you wherever beauty is done,
>   or truth is told,
>   or lovers whisper.
> God is there, looking back everywhere, in everything.
>   You are seen. See!
>   You are seen. Sing!

So that is my story, my crazy bird friends. And that is my invitation. Oh, this day, this very day, let your bird brains take over. Thinking is fine except when it does not acknowledge its own limitations. When you reach those limitations, follow your craziness. Fly in that vast inner space that stretches within you as far as the heavens stretch without. Fly to the stable of that baby Jesus who was all eyes. Fly and sing!

Yes, of course it may seem there are more reasons not to sing than to sing. But there is one reason to sing, one small, unshakable, unconquerable reason to sing: it is that baby who grew to be a man, who insisted with his life that God has an eye on you, on us, an eye that will never lose us in the dark. Oh, brothers and sisters, that is our story to sing. You are seen! What matters is the singing of that song. Courage, then. Dare to sing it!

And Now

Shadow and Gold
The Birthmark and the Scent
Gum on the Altar

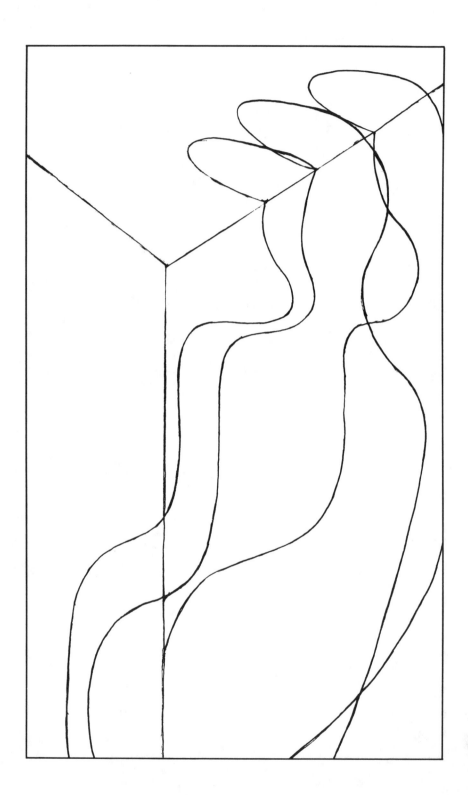

Shadow and Gold

He'd been driving for several hours, since shortly after the church service that morning. He had made no plans, but as soon as the reception was over, he'd simply gotten into his car and begun to drive. But plans or not, something in him must have known where he had to go, though it had been more years than he could remember since he had been there. He'd been on the Interstate driving west for several hours before he realized, or admitted, that he was going back. When he'd come over the mountains and down through the rolling hill country onto the prairies, his heart had suddenly quickened. It was as it always had been, spinning off toward the horizon and going on forever. The land hadn't changed. There was something timeless in its being so bare and flat, being so essentially and simply what it was and nothing else, naked and unashamed. On the plains the eye could see the sun sink at the edge of the world, and nothing hindered the wind.

He had thought to himself, "Every valley shall be lifted up, and every mountain and hill be made low; the uneven ground shall become level and the rough places a plain. And the glory of the Lord shall be revealed and the flesh shall see it together."

He'd smiled ruefully. There was more nostalgia than expectation in those words for him. Valleys might be lifted up and mountains made low; the plains country testified to that possibility. But who would turn time back? Who would make his flesh young again? The glory of the Lord had better hurry in its revelation.

He left the Interstate and drove on the arrow-straight two-lane blacktop road that divided the sections of farmland like squares on a checker board. It was Sunday night, and he only met an occasional car. He went through two or three small towns where apparently everyone was inside, everything closed, and the streets empty. It was not at all like his city. He began to feel very alone; or was it just that he was unable now, in this vast emptiness which disguised nothing, to avoid the fact of his aloneness?

The wind rocked his car, sometimes nearly forcing it off the road. It was cold, bitterly cold this December night. There is something about that kind of cold that forces a person inward. He noticed, too, that the cold did seem to freeze into place the battle lines between the darkness and the lights on the farmhouse porches and in their windows. There was a certain sharpness where the light and darkness met, or separated, a sharpness and fragileness, as if of an uneasy truce. Here and there a family had hung Christmas lights outside on some leafless tree where, being so isolated, they seemed more forlorn than festive.

He thought about that morning in his church. "What did I say?" he muttered aloud in arising panic. "Christ, maybe I've got Alzheimer's. I can't even remember my own sermons any more. They all run together in a blur."

Even the faces at the reception had been a blur. Every year they gave him a Christmas gift, something of an embarrassment to everyone, a tradition no one knew how to stop. Michael Judkins had made the presentation and said something about this being the minister's twenty-fifth year with them and how they hoped there would be twenty-five more. On cue the blur had murmured and clapped. Then hands had reached out to shake his. Finally, he'd gotten in the car and started to drive, blindly but with angry determination. They knew he had to retire in the spring. Were they mocking him with that twenty-five-years-more talk? He reached into his coat pocket where he'd tucked the envelope without looking at it. He wasn't even sure he'd said thank you. He pulled out the envelope and held it in the glow of the dash board: "To John Paulson. Minister of Trinity Church for Twenty-Five Fruitful Years. Merry Christmas."

"Fruitful? Good God, if only they knew," John mused to himself. "Some words should be stricken from the language."

Off to the left he saw a bonfire. Probably it was at the edge of a frozen pond where ice-skaters came to warm themselves. He remembered such fires as a boy. And he remembered his grandfather telling him that during a flu epidemic back sometime, somewhere, the grave diggers buried the dead at night, digging graves beside just such fires so they could see what they were digging. Night burials prevented the spread of germs, the old man had said, nodding his head wisely and winking at him.

He'd never forgotten that image, one of so many frightened memories he carried from his past, but one that seemed to capture the terror of all the others. Death and darkness were all mixed up in it, along with something about disease and corruption and punishment, and people dying because they were bad, or bad because they were dying. So you had to be . . . what? Or do . . . what? What? Some extraordinary thing or you'd die or . . . something. It was all so confusing. In his head he knew it was absurd, but the feeling was adhesive and powerful. He'd been driven by it all his life. He'd tried so hard, so desperately hard, to do something, to be . . .

"To be WHAT?" he yelled at the darkness, hitting the steering wheel with his fist. What the goddamnhell was it he was trying to be all this damn time? Innocent? Maybe that was it. Maybe innocence would make a person invincible, immune to the darkness, to the grave with the fires burning alongside and the shadows dancing mockingly all around? What would make a person invincible? It was a ridiculous question, he knew. But such an urgent one. After all, why had he chosen to be a minister? What had he been looking for? Why was he going back now, after all these years, back in space as if that were a way to go back in time? It was his own flight into Egypt, a flight not to escape some Herodic danger, but an attempt to go back to where the captivity had started. If one is ever to be delivered, maybe one has to go back to where the bondage began in order to discover how it had happened, what went wrong. Maybe that was really why Joseph and Mary took Jesus to Egypt. At least Joseph had the gold the wisemen had given them to pay for their stay, to keep Jesus safe while those other babies got slaughtered.

Even if the story was only symbolic, as most scholars insisted, the question was still, "Symbolic of what?" Maybe gold is symbolic of safety. Maybe it's money that makes one invincible, at least as invincible as a mortal can be. Well, at least he had what they'd given him at the reception, which usually was about $500 or so. And he still had the $10,000 he had gotten from her life insurance policy when Alice had died three years ago. It wasn't much, which might explain why he didn't feel invincible. He shrugged and shifted in his seat.

The snow suddenly came more fiercely; a few flakes warning, then, before the warning could be heeded, the full storm—quick, blinding, inundating the road, the fence rows, all the landmarks in a raging sea of white. The flakes assaulted him straight on, then went wind-driven sideways, giving him the sensation that the world had suddenly been tilted on edge, and he and the car would fall and go tumbling off into space. He clutched at the steering wheel. The snow was hypnotic. He crept along, squinting through the mounds of snow the wipers piled on either side of the small semi-circle through which he peered.

The irony of the situation struck him: he would not be buried in a grave attended by leaping flames after all, but under mountains of whiteness and the eerie silence that always follows howling blizzards. He was surprised that he was less afraid than curious about the possibility. He smiled, and it occurred to him that God must have a sense of humor, a thought which made him wonder if he was going mad. The whole circumstance of his being there at all, and no one knowing, was quite absurd.

"But," he said half aloud, as though sound would keep the snow at bay, "what does reason have to do with anything? Life isn't rational. Or maybe it is, and I'm not. Madness! Is it me or . . . what? I start looking for something and even though I'm not sure exactly what it is, what happens? Every possible clue gets buried under a pile of snow—time, space, everything. What else could it be but madness, or God's joke. I hope he's laughing."

He rolled down his window, put his head out and screamed. He'd begun to perspire, and his head ached. The air felt good, and the scream. Then, quickly, it was too cold. The snow stuck on his eye lashes, and he couldn't see. He pulled his head in and rolled his window halfway up. Something in him wanted to give up, just stop and let the snow take him in whatever way it would. But something deeper in him urged him to go on. Why?

He edged the car ahead slowly, feeling his way more than seeing it, as a person gropes with a foot for the top stair in a dark, unfamiliar house, hoping to find it before tumbling down the whole flight. A hundred yards, two hundred, five hundred in how many minutes . . . ten? . . . fifteen? Then, into the swirl of white floated a large billboard, flood lit, startling, ghostly. "Peace on Earth," it said in huge red letters. "Holiday Greetings from Hamilton. Welcome to the home of the State Champion Flying Falcons." Memories came flooding in before he could shut the gates. Somewhere in his attic, or basement, there was a box with a trophy in it, and a photograph in brown tint of a team of smooth-cheeked, wrinkled-uniformed boys in awkward pose, and a sweater with a large H sewn on it with a great winged bird soaring on the crosspiece.

Another hundred feet or so and his car skidded and stalled. He sat in the darkness and could not stop the flow of memories. So long ago, yet like yesterday it was. There had been a party. Someone had gotten some beer, even though they were minors and laws were strictly obeyed in those days in that small town. There had been girls, and laughter, and dancing, and what they euphemistically called "necking"—though necks were about the only body part not much involved. There had also been a gnawing anxiety in the pit of his stomach. It had gotten late. He was driving his family's old Ford. It might have happened on this very road. He'd been half-asleep, after taking Jody McFarland home out by Salt Creek. He was by himself. There'd been a sharp, loud bump. Had it been a sudden rut in the road, a rock, maybe . . . something . . . a dog, a calf? Had something moved, off to the right just before the bump, or was it a shadow, a dream figure? He had been jolted awake, his heart pounding, but he hadn't stopped.

The next day there had been a small piece in the paper and some talk about a hit-and-run accident on Salt Creek Road. Some Negro girl was in the hospital, badly hurt. But she'd live, they said, and it didn't matter much, really, since she was a Negro. He'd gone home and looked over the Ford carefully. He couldn't see any marks or dents. Still, that could have been the bump he'd felt. He had said nothing, out of fear. Talk passed. The police gave up the investigation. But for weeks he'd had trouble sleeping.

Along with the terrible chance that he was guilty of a hit-and-run accident was the feeling that he was guilty of so many other things as well: cheating on exams, sometimes; telling lies to excuse himself, or impress people; his burning interest in sex and masturbating; his sexual "experiments" with Jody, which they always managed to stop just short of losing their technical virginity; his drinking beer with his friends when his mother was so much against it; his very average grades which so disappointed his parents. So with the "possible accident" on Salt Creek Road came the growing certainty that he was just not good enough. Something was definitely wrong with him. That was the feeling he couldn't get rid of. It was always there in the shadows of his life, waiting until the laughter had died out, and the awards were stored on the shelf, and the last person had gone home, and the final duty done, and the wine glasses emptied, and the late show flickered away and the last prayers said. And then, there it was: not good enough, not good enough. In his dreams was the recurring image of the fires, and the ghoulish grave diggers burying people at night to prevent the spread of germs, or corruption. What huge shadows the grave diggers must have cast across the land as they dug beside the fires. He'd seen those shadows in his dreams. Had they laughed as they worked? Did everyone know some joke he didn't?

"What the hell do I want? What am I looking for? God help me!" he cried. "They'll find me buried in this car, and they'll never know the real reason I'm here. I don't even know myself."

The snow began to pile up around the car. Finally, in a burst of resolve, he got out and began walking. The snow was drifting and filled his shoes. He pulled up his coat collar against the wind. The snow was falling in finer grain now, abating somewhat. But the cold was relentless and penetrating. There were a few scattered houses, then a few more, then a street sign with a name he didn't recognize. It had been nearly forty years since he'd been back. He didn't know what part of town he was in, or where he was going. The houses looked warm and friendly. He imagined scenes of tranquility and happiness in each one. Something in him believed those ads. There was a way it was supposed to be—clean, neat, combed, and radiant. He just had never found it.

The cold was numbing. He came to an intersection. The stop light swung and bounced in the wind. Cars with chains crunched slowly down the street. Suddenly it all seemed familiar to him—these streets, the feel of this town, this past. He'd always walked alone, even as a boy.

Another corner. There was the big, brick Presbyterian Church standing as stolidly as ever, an anchor for the town against the storms of wind and dust and frivolity. He'd grown up in it. Even as a boy he intuitively understood the solemn tones of the church, its drama with all the parts so unctuously played, that symbiosis of pulpit and pew. Yet, he also sensed the stifling fraud of it, and of himself in it, as well. Why did anyone take part in it? Why did he? Even as a teenager he felt the church suck out people's juice and spit it to the wind. Where was the praise, the wonder, the joy that was supposed to be part of it?

The snow had stopped, but the wind had not. It never did. Which way should he go? How would he know if he found what he had come for? He felt disoriented, queasy. Which way was the old house? He started walking in what he decided was the right direction. He thought he recognized a house along the way, but then everything began to look strange and unfamiliar. Had he made a wrong turn? He walked doggedly on. In the next block a bar was open. He went in. "White Christmas" was playing on the juke box. Two men watched the TV flickering on a shelf along one wall. The bartender moved toward him.

He felt foolish. "Kline Street. I'm looking for Kline Street.

Which way is it?" The bartender laughed, wiped his nose on his apron, and told him Kline Street was way the hell over on the other side of town. John shrugged and left.

He was beginning to feel desperate. It was so cold. He remembered delivering papers at 4 A.M. on Sunday when it was way below zero, pulling the heavy papers along on his sled, and coming home shivering, and his father being proud of him and cooking him bacon and eggs for breakfast. It was one of the few times he'd pleased his father, much as he kept trying.

Then he heard music. It was coming from a run-down, clapboard building. "The Holiness Gospel, Assembly of God in Christ, Everyone Welcome," the sign in front read. He stood on the steps and listened to them sing. "God is blessing me right now, right now." The words were simple, and the singers repeated them over and over. He pushed the door open a crack to look in. The door bumped a man standing right there. The man opened the door wide and motioned him in. John hunched his shoulders and went in, feeling trapped.

It was a small place, somehow disheveled looking. There were no pews, just folding chairs, and people crowded together in uneven rows. He sat and tried to scrunch down inconspicuously, but people kept smiling at him. Another blur. Small as the place was, the preacher used a hand microphone. His voice blared but the words came out muffled, and John could only make out some of them: " . . . listen, brothers and sisters . . . to the Word of God . . . Let it seep down and fill your soul. Hear . . . unto your salvation . . . God's Word . . . sharper than a two-edged sword . . . burns like fire to purge away the chaff . . . eternal damnation . . ." On all sides a rising chorus of "Amen" and "Preach" and "Thank You, Jesus" sounded in antiphonal rhythm with the preacher, who went thundering on: "Hear what Saint Matthew has written: 'As were the days of Noah, so will be the coming of the Son of man . . . they did not know until the flood came and swept them all away.' Do you know what that meeeans?" the preacher exhorted, sucking in air before going on.

As John watched and listened, the room began to spin and tilt. It was hot, and the man's words pounded at him, battered him. What had brought him to this place? Was this somehow what he was meant to hear? He felt sick. The preacher crescendoed on: "It meeeeans that

Jeeessuus is coming as a flood to sweeeep away the wrooong-doers, the adulterers, the for-ni-caa-tors ... the cheats ... the drunks and the puuur-verts ... those who cooovet what is their neighbor's ... break the commandments ... Repent! Repent, I say, reeee-pent!"

John stood, groped along the wall and rushed out into the night, running until the coldness tore at his lungs and the pain of it was too much. "Do you know what that means? Do you know?" the preacher had shouted. Do you know, do you know, do you know? Did that preacher know? Did anyone? Was God really so obvious to some, so obscure to others? He staggered and began to cry, great wracking sobs: "Repent! Repent! Of what? Of what? What did I come back here for?"

He had reached the edge of town. On the left he recognized the little cemetery where his parents were buried. He turned toward it, but it was blocked by a large snow drift. Suddenly he was just too tired. He sank to his knees. Then he sat with a sigh and leaned against the snow drift. Some fifty yards away was the Paulson family plot, the snow pulled up over it like a great comforter.

On an impulse he pulled out the envelope the church had given him and tore it open. His fingers were numb, stiff in the cold. But somehow there was just enough light to see, as if the snow was its source. Good God, was he seeing things? No, there were thousand dollar bills in the envelope. He began counting: "Seven, eight, nine ... Oh my God! What have they done! Thirteen, fourteen, fifteen . . . What could Judkins really have meant about wishing I'd have twenty-five more years with them? This must be a going away present ... nineteen, twenty ... Is there a note with it? No. I don't see one. Twenty-one, twenty-two . . . What are they saying to me? Twenty-four, twenty-five ... twenty-five thousand dollars and I ran ... I don't remember even saying thank you ..." He was mumbling now, looking at the dark sky, imploring.

Then he began to cry again. He felt alone, lost, tired, a foolish old man. Suddenly he felt warm and sleepy. It was a pleasant feeling. He wondered what happened to bodies no one claimed. Would anyone be looking for him, report him as missing? It didn't matter, he guessed. It was time to sleep.

"Hey, wake up, man." The voice came from a distance, but he

couldn't open his eyes to locate it. He wanted it to go away. It didn't.

"What are you doin' there? Scared me half to death. You gonna freeze stiff as a board you don't get up, get movin'. You hear? Man, what are you doin' wi' thall that money? You rob a bank or somethin'? Here, just let me help you wi' that. Now, come on! Wake up! Wake up!"

The voice was floating down to him from somewhere way off. He tried again to open his eyes. This time he managed. The blur came slowly into focus and became a very black face and a head wrapped in a scarf.

"Who are you?" he rasped. "A grave digger? That must be who. A gravedigger."

"I ain't no grave digger," mouthed the black face. "I been accused of bein' a gold digger but never no grave digger. You want one of them, you gotta wait a long time. Gotta wait'll the ground gets warm again. Folks round here call me C.J. 'cause my name's Christina Juliet. Lived in Hamilton all my life. I been follahin' you since you left the Assembly Hall back there. I figured a stranger as wild lookin' as you either be in some kinda trouble or lookin' for some. Either way, somebody gonna need help. So I follah'd you. Only I can't go too fast, so I lost you for awhile. So I just walked after your tracks in the snow till I found you. Now come on, get up 'fore we both freeze to death."

She took his arm and helped him to his feet. He looked dis-believingly at her.

"Come on, come on," said C.J. "I don't live too far from here. My place ain't much, but it's a whole lot warmer 'n this."

They walked slowly, leaning on each other, shuffling through the snow to the little house on the street facing the other side of the cemetery. It was absolutely the last house in town, or the first house on the prairie. They went in.

"Now you just lay down on this here couch," C.J. gasped, lifting his arm from her shoulder and easing him down. "That's it. I'll get some wood for the stove. And light the lamp. Electricity don't come this far."

It was an old Franklin stove like his grandmother's. She got the fire going quickly, but she seemed to forget about the lamp. He watched her without saying a word. When the wood was burning nicely, she reached in a gunny sack and got a few pieces of coal and tossed them in the stove door. The shadows moved in strange patterns across the wall and the ceiling as she worked. Finally satisfied, she shut the door, reached down and adjusted some vents, then reached up and turned the damper just so. Then she put a hand inside her coat, pulled out the envelope and put it on a little table next to the rocker where she sat down.

"There's a whole lot of green stuff there, man," said C.J. "What was you doin' sittin' there in the snow, holdin' it like you was? Who was you offerin' it to? I don't mind telling you I was sorely tempted to just relieve you of it and leave you there . . . sleepin'. I done a lot a things I'm not much proud of to get a lot less money than that. And if I'da done it, just took th' money and left you, nobody woulda known. There's enough there to take care of me for quite a spell, Lord knows."

He felt a creeping lassitude. "So why didn't you?" he murmured.

"Lord, that's a good question," she chuckled. "I mulled it awhile, all right, watchin' you 'bout to doze off to Beulah Land, and then it come to me that the Lord was testin' me."

"Testing you? The Lord? How's that?" John pushed himself up.

"Oh my, yes indeed!" she replied, chuckling louder. "The Lord was testin' me to see if I be trustworthy. In little things . . . so's He know if I be fit for glory."

"You go to that . . . to the Assembly of God . . . whatever it's called . . . where I was when you started following me?"

"Sometimes," C.J. nodded. "While ago, more than recent. Mostly I backslide. 'Cept round Christmas, like now, and Easter. But the Book say the Lord is wed to backsliders, too, sure 'nuff, which is comfortin' . . . 'cept to them what don't backslide. Howsoever, maybe I backslided 'cause I never got saved."

John sat up and leaned forward. "How do you know you never got saved?"

"Well, I never got the Spirit, that's how," replied C.J. "I know the Book, all right, and I was regular at services and all. But I just never got the Spirit."

"But how do you know if you got the Spirit or not? What does that mean? I mean, you seem . . . saved enough to me. You didn't let me freeze. You saved me, didn't you? Isn't that . . . doesn't that count . . . for something?" John was struggling. Why was he asking this woman about things like this anyway?

"Bless my soul," C.J. said, rocking back and forth. "Don't you know nothin' about the Spirit? I'll tell you. It's like this. First there's the savin' Spirit. You get that, you know, repentin' regular, and gettin' baptized and goin' to prayer meetin' and all that. You get that regular. But after that, you got to get the holdin' Spirit. See, there's the savin' Spirit and then there's the holdin' Spirit. Most folks can get the savin' Spirit, no trouble. It's the holdin' Spirit that's hard to get. For that, you got to tarry."

"Tarry?" John frowned. "What's that?"

"Tarry? You don't know tarry?" C.J. asked incredulously. "Plain to see you not much for knowin' the ways of the Spirit. It's in the Book where Jesus say to his disciples, 'Come and tarry awhile with me.' See, you got to tarry to get the flesh willin', like the Spirit's willin'. You got to tarry down on your knees all night, and readin' the Book, and lovin' your neighbor . . . and not just once in awhile when you feelin' up to it. You got to do all that to get the holdin' Spirit. Get the holdin' Spirit, and you're really saved. Sanc-ti-fied." She emphasized each syllable solemnly. "Be a deacon, then."

"Well," John replied, "maybe the holding Spirit comes before the saving Spirit. Ever think of that?"

"Now what you mean, sayin' a silly thing like that?" she scolded.

Suddenly he felt flustered, as though rubbing two words together with an idea was altogether beyond him in the face of such simple wisdom. Finally he gathered himself, took a deep breath and said, "Well, maybe God's got a hold of you all the time, even when you don't know it . . . or believe it much . . . or often. I mean, why else would you . . . would I . . . be looking for . . . for . . ."

"Lookin' for what?" asked C.J.

"Looking for . . . for anything," he managed to say. "You know, looking for salvation. Maybe if you're looking for it, want something enough, you already have it, or . . . some of it anyway. And sometimes you are aware of it . . . a little. You know?"

She rocked and studied him for a long time. Then she asked, "What's your name?"

"John Paulson"

"Ah! I thought you looked familiar," C.J. exclaimed. "You used to live in this town, didn't you?"

"It was a long time ago," he replied, warily.

"But I 'member you. I was in your class at school. You wouldna recollected me now 'cause you certainly never paid me no mind then. Sure 'nuff, nobody did. This town is like all the rest when it comes to black folks. Besides, you was a big hero."

John looked at her carefully and felt his gut tighten. "You . . . walk with a limp. I think I . . . would remember that. It's not a big town, you know. I mean . . . people notice something like that. What . . . caused it? Did you get . . . have polio or something? As a kid. Are you sure you remember me? Really?"

"Oh my, yes, I 'member you clear as anythin'. But course you don't recollect me 'cause I didn't have a limp then. I got hit one night my last year in high school. Hit-and-run driver. I almost died."

He started to shiver and sweat. The room suddenly seemed more than silent. The fire danced in the stove and shadows played on the ceiling overhead, a thousand shapes, a thousand demons. His mouth was dry. All that time, all that way and now here it was. Here she was. He couldn't begin to unravel how or why, of all the possibilities, this night, this place had happened. At last he whispered, "I . . . may have been . . . that hit-and-run driver."

"You?" The rocking stopped. The fire reflected in her eyes. He held his breath. She closed her eyes. The rocking resumed.

"Yes, me. I don't know if I . . . hit anyone or not. There was just this bump. I was half asleep. I didn't stop. I went on home. Then the next morning I heard. About the accident," he explained. He was shaking.

"Oh my God!" C.J. moaned. She stopped rocking, leaned toward him and studied his face for a long time. He tried to return her gaze, but couldn't. He shifted his eyes to the fire.

The only sound was the wind. Then she began to rock again,

making a slow squeak.

"She knows," he thought to himself. "She knows I'm the one. Now it's all up to her."

"What if I was . . . the one?" he whispered.

"That'd be some coincidence, wouldn't it?" C.J. replied softly. By some strange alchemy, everything about her seemed to have consolidated, drawn inward and gone deep past following. "Or maybe it be somethin' more than a coincidence. More mysterious than that. At first, layin' there in the hospital all those weeks, I wanted to kill that driver. But after awhile that feelin' passed. I figured whoever it was must have had what he done gnawin' inside of him, tormentin' him terrible and would as long as he lived. And I didn't want it gnawin' inside me like that. So I decided I'd forgive whoever it was. For both our sakes."

He looked over at her. Her head was back, her eyes closed. She rocked slowly back and forth, from shadow to light, from black to gold.

"Do you . . . forgive me now? Face to face?" asked John.

"Oh, yes, yes. I forgive you for whatever you need bein' forgiven for. But it ain't the hit-and-run you need forgivin' for, really," C.J. answered.

"No? I thought . . . I mean . . . . What are you saying?"

"Well, when I thought about it, just now," C.J. chuckled, "I recollected that it was one of them open-back, old delivery trucks that hit me. Your family never had no truck, did they?"

"No, but . . . but then what are you forgiving me for?" he asked.

"Well, the way I see it, you need forgivin' more for miss-and-run than hit-and-run. You never paid me no mind in school, nor a lot of other things neither. First I figured it was just another case of white folks stupidity and uppity. Then I seen it was 'cause you was so scared, somehow. Fear, or somethin' like that, put a cloud in your eyes. I bet you've missed more than half your life, livin' like that, runnin' scared all the time. Oh my, yes, miss-and-run. That's what you need forgivin' for. So, I forgives you and you is forgiven. Just like that. Guess the Lord done give me that power when the Spirit say to follah you from the Assembly. So now you don't no mo' gotta keep missin' who you is by tryin' to be somethin' you ain't."

There was only the squeak of the rocker and the whistle of the wind and the glow of the fire, soft and easy in the room, making the shadows friendly. He wondered if C.J. might not be telling the truth about what really happened, about being hit by a truck. But at the same time he realized it wasn't really innocence or invincibility he'd wanted or needed. It was deliverance, a kind of self-acceptance. And she was right. What he really needed deliverance from was miss-and-run, because that was exactly what he'd been doing all his life. Maybe he could try something else.

"Would you . . . would you come and lie down and hold me?" he asked. He felt awkward in asking and didn't look at her. But after a moment, he did look at her and smiled. She was studying him thoughtfully.

He talked on to hide his embarassment. "Look, when I came here, back to this town . . . I really didn't know why. At least not so I was aware of it. I was looking for something, but I didn't know exactly what. Maybe it was you. Or maybe it was . . . an angel. Like the ones who told the shepherds not to be afraid when Jesus was born. Anyway, I think I found . . . both."

"I ain't no angel," C.J. protested.

"Maybe not," he smiled. "Maybe not. But whatever you are, you're . . . okay. More than okay. Fit for glory. And I am glad I found you. Would you . . . please . . . hold me? Let me hold you, for awhile?"

At last she limped out of the shadows and across the little room and laid down. They held each other then like small children. After a time she spoke softly. "Maybe you be on to somethin' 'bout the holdin' power of the Spirit, I mean 'bout wantin' bein' a real good way toward havin'. I mean, maybe you really be on to somethin' there."

The fire held steady, and the only sounds beside the wind were giggles, the hum of the fire, and sometimes the squeak of the rocker as if someone were sitting in it, watching.

When he left quietly in the first light of dawn, before C.J. was awake, the money was snuggled on the little table next to the rocker, which seemed to move ever so slightly back and forth, even though there was no wind—only an utter, awesome, blue-domed, white silence. She opened an eye, watched him go, knowing he'd be back sometime; and a very peaceful smile trickled off her face onto the pillow as she turned back to sleep, to dream.

"Therefore you also must be ready. For the son of man is coming at an hour you do not expect." *

*Matthew 24:44, RSV

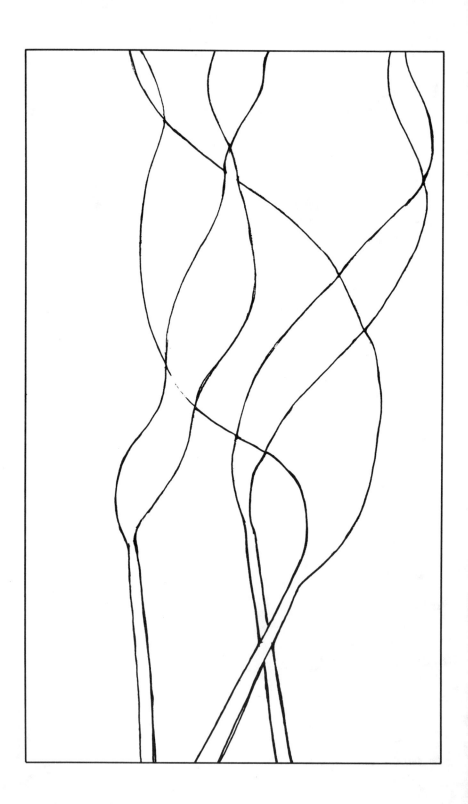

The Birthmark
and the Scent

She ran her hand through her disheveled hair and watched through the kitchen window as the darkness slowly turned grey. There was ice on the inside of the panes of glass, residue of a cold night. The ice seemed fitting, somehow, for this day, this decisive day. Her fingers touched her cheek.

"Damn birthmark," she muttered. "Why the hell did anyone ever call it that anyway? Death mark is what it is. Damn it anyway. Damn God. Damn 'em all. Do you hear it? Damn you, God! Damn you, damn you!"

Her hands gripped the sink. She stared at the drain and felt suddenly sick to her stomach. The birthmark was the liver-colored blotch along the left side of her face and down her neck trickling onto her breast. She wore turtlenecks to cover as much as she could of it.

"God's bloody fingerprint. Why didn't you keep your fumbling hands off me?" she snarled.

God's bloody fingerprint, that's what she'd come to call it, had called it for what seemed forever, though she was only forty-two years old. It didn't matter. For her there was no past when it had not been, no future when it would not be. She was branded and that was that. Branded, but unclaimed. Unwanted. It was too much.

She re-tied the belt on her terry cloth robe, picked up her coffee and padded out of the kitchen. In the small living room she took several sticks of incense out of a box, put them in holders around the room and lit them. It took her five minutes. When she finished, she inhaled deeply, sank down on the couch and curled her feet under her. She laid her head back. She loved the smell of incense, the atmosphere it created for her—dreamy, mysterious, yet safe. The scent entered her, became part of her, blurred the harshness, bore her away. With the smell came memories, inevitably, memories of long ago, of a little girl with her parents in a very large church, tracing the carvings on the ends of the wooden pews, gazing awed at the great high window over the altar, hearing the bells tinkle and the beautiful priest in the white gown swinging the smoking censer on a gold chain and the chanting. She could hear it still:

" 'I'll call upon thee, O Lord . . . let my prayer be counted as incense before thee . . . the lifting up of my hands as a . . . sacrifice.' Sweet Jesus, after all these years, I still remember it. Why? Why? It never made any difference . . . not the slightest . . . even to them. Did Dad and Mom believe it then? Do they now? Good Catholics. Will they forgive me? Ever?"

The birthmark was the indelible fact around which her life came to be organized, or disorganized. Nothing could change that. She remembered the antiseptic smell of endless doctors' offices. One after another they'd said there was nothing they could do, no cosmetic surgery, nothing. The birthmark was too massive. Nothing could work.

"Nothing!" she whispered emphatically. "Ergo, the abyss, the eternal void. The great cosmic emptiness."

Somewhere in that succession of examinations, of doctors' hushed conferences with her grim-faced parents, and then the ice cream cones and too-loud talk and too-easy laughter afterward, she'd come to the realization that she was different, an embarrassment, that there was something wrong, hopelessly wrong. It frightened her, but she could not talk about her fear because she sensed that her birthmark had also become the blight around which her family's life was oriented, or disoriented. Despite medical reassurances, her parents had decided against having more children. She was an only child.

"One freak was enough, right?" She spat the words at the photographs on the mantel. "Why didn't you just say it and be done with it? My God, all the deceit, all the phoniness. Oh Daddy, why?"

When he came home from work, her father would talk of everything else: "How's Daddy's sweet princess today? Were you a good girl? Did you have fun playing? Did you help your Mommy?"

But he never looked at her.

"How was school today, princess?" her father would go on automatically. "Did you do well? Did you study hard? I'll just bet you're the smartest one in the whole class."

But he never really looked at her.

When she was older, he would tell her, "I know you'll do well at the university, princess. I'm so proud of you. You've never given me a moment's worry, like so many other daughters give their parents."

She sipped her coffee and grunted at the memory: "No, no worry. My God, what would you worry about? What could be more embarrassing than the way I looked? My losing my virginity? Getting pregnant? Is that what you meant? What else, right? Did it ever occur to you to wonder what I felt? Who the hell would want a disfigured female? Isn't that why you never worried? What about me? Oh, I had dates, all right. With those stiff junior high school boys whose parents felt sorry for me and told their sons to be nice to me, like little gentlemen. Just more vomitus condescension. But the kids tried, they really did. And we all survived and went to high school where there were always boys who believed, as they said, that if you put a sack over our heads, you couldn't tell one female from another. And who could see a blotch in the back seat when it was dark anyway? They figured I'd be grateful for their attention so I'd be easy and . . . NO WORRY? MY GOD. YOU NEVER REALLY LOOKED AT ME!"

Her father talked of everything else. Her mother talked of little else: "Poor dear. Mother's poor, sweet dear. But you must remember that beauty is only skin deep, Jane. That's all. Just skin deep."

Cynically, Jane thought, "Yes, of course. But why all those creams and lotions, mother? Why were you always soaking in the bathtub and looking in every mirror you passed, straightening your seams and brushing the dandruff off?"

Her mother would say with a sort of rehearsed earnestness, "You see, dear, you can overcome this . . . unfortunate handicap. We do want the very best for you, dear; your happiness is what matters to us. Just remember, most men do appreciate a good listener, and many will seek out a woman with a pleasing personality. You can cultivate those traits, you see?"

Jane whispered tearfully, "You were beautiful, Mom. As a little girl I watched you put on make-up and perfume, and style your hair, and I wondered if I could learn how to . . . to hide my blemish, be beautiful, like you. Did you ever think that I might want to be like you?"

Her mother's voice flooded in again: "Style is so important, dear. How you dress, the colors you choose. You have to accentuate the positive things, dear, and disguise the negative. Carriage is critical, how you walk. You have to create a total impression. Total impression is what matters."

Jane sighed, "I finally realized you were talking about packaging, merchandising. Appearances. A good front. But why, Mom, why? What did you want? Is that all you were about, attracting men? Why?"

The tape of her mother's voice went on in her head, oblivious to the question: "I'm sure you can make a good life for yourself, Jane, in spite of everything. You can find something useful to do. God wants us to be useful, you know, to live for others, forget ourselves. Perhaps you can find something in research, working in a laboratory or something. Or a librarian, perhaps."

"SHUT UP!" Jane screamed. "JUST SHUT THE HELL UP! I was your frigging problem, wasn't I? Your blemish, your burden, your embarrassment! Why? Why? I was your DAUGHTER, FOR GOD'S SAKE . . . your flesh and blood daughter . . . and it didn't turn out like it was supposed to, did it, like the movies . . . WHERE WERE YOU, MOTHER? WHO . . . oh my God. It doesn't matter any more. It doesn't matter."

She got up and went to the window. The sky was blue now, a clear cold morning. Across the way Mrs. Dowling was retrieving her newspaper. Next to her, the Burgesses had put up their big evergreen wreath on the front door. Christmas was nearly here. She wondered what they would think when they found her. "All for the best," they'd probably say, shaking their heads knowingly, desperately trying to avoid the stark reality of it, as people always avoid something ugly and frightening. She turned from the window. Her foot kicked a book that was lying on the floor where she'd left it. It was her high school yearbook, lying next to a cardboard box full of pictures and scrapbooks. She'd gotten them out and looked at them through the night. She knelt by the box and picked up something that caught her eye.

"Jane Bradley," she read. "Third Grade Report Card. Spring. Mrs. Wolf, teacher. Reading, A; Arithmetic, A; Geography, A; Deportment, A. Comment: 'Jane is a model student. We love having her in our class.' We? Our? Who was she talking about? Wasn't it my class, too? Did you take a poll, Mrs. Wolf, to find out how many loved having me in their class?"

She picked up a photograph. It was a grammar school class. She spotted herself, carefully placed in the third row, on the end, turned so her birthmark wouldn't show. She remembered the day, how she'd wanted to cry but didn't, how solicitous the teacher had been. She put the photograph down and picked up the yearbook. She turned to her picture, there on the page with the seniors whose names began with B. It was full face, her head held high, the birthmark clearly visible. She'd been defiant in those years.

She remembered her adviser her first year of high school. Lucille Barth was her name, pert and bright and oh so helpfully serious. She said: "Jane, self-pity is an obnoxious trait. You must never feel sorry for yourself. So many people are so much worse off than you. People are blind or retarded or terribly crippled or have perfectly awful diseases. You have so much going for you. You can overcome your problem if you'll just work and use your brains.

Achievement, Jane. That's what matters. Achievement! I'll help you. Count on me. Come in and talk to me anytime."

"Oh, right!" Jane scoffed, "achievement does it everytime." She read the legend under her Senior picture: "Jane Bradley—Voted Miss Inspirational. Honor Society; Pep Club; Debate Team—First place district tournament three years running; Journalism; Business Manager, The Scroll; Glee Club; Stage Manager of Thespians . . . College Bound." She graduated at the top of her class.

The Saturday after graduation, Lucille Barth married the high school principal, Mr. Watson. Four senior girls were attendants. Jane was not invited. A week later, Lucille Barth Watson wrote an apology. It was an oversight, she'd written, a stupid, unforgivable oversight. She signed the letter, "Your friend always, Lucille B. Watson." Three weeks after graduation, Jane was in the hospital. She couldn't keep anything down. All the tests were negative. She still wouldn't eat. She became more and more depressed. They took her, finally, to a psychiatrist.

"Russell Smalls, M.D." it said on the tasteful name plate next to the door of his paneled office. Jane reminisced aloud, "One hundred dollars a visit. For what?" She recalled her only appointment.

"When did you first feel depressed, Jane?" he'd asked.

"In third grade," she'd responded.

"In third grade? What happened in the third grade? Anything special?"

"Actually, it didn't happen then."

"And what was it that happened?" he inquired professionally.

"My birthmark," she'd said. "Obviously."

"I see."

"I'm sure you do," she'd flipped back at him.

"You seem angry."

"Maybe," she'd sighed, trying to stay controlled. "I don't know."

"When were you first aware of your birthmark?"

"I don't know. I don't want to talk about it."

"Why not?"

"Because it won't help!"

"What would help?"

"I don't know." She'd teared up in spite of herself. "Maybe it would help for all these questions to stop."

"All right. Why don't you ask the questions?"

Without thinking she'd yelled: "WHY DO I HAVE THIS DAMN BIRTHMARK?"

"That is an interesting question. What do you think?"

"Oh my God," she'd moaned, tears running down her cheeks.

"What about God?"

She was sobbing. "Yes . . . what about . . . God?" She didn't go back.

But by the end of the summer, she'd felt good enough to attend the university. It was a turbulent time. She threw herself into it. The civil rights movement. The anti-war movement. Jeans and sweat shirts and long hair and unisex. They marched. They protested. They talked. They sang, "The times, they are a-changin'." They had the world by the tail. It was a time to change things, to throw out old values. They listened to rock, and slept together, and then they just split, moved on.

"Split," Jane remembered. "That was it. Nothing changed. People got shot, assassinated. The war went on. And we just split. SPLIT. 'See ya' around.' 'Catch ya' later.' 'It's been real.' Real? My God, what's real? The world was just like it had always been, probably always would be. And there was God's bloody fingerprint on me. And everybody just split."

She was a language major. She'd turned to poetry. She reached into the box and rummaged for her old notebook. She found it, opened it, flipped through the pages, started reading:

"Time heaves us into awareness with a heedless roar;
spawned within the cosmic sea, tossed upon this track-
less shore,
we're cast as orphans on this infinitesimal dot
like shipwrecked denizens on some barren rock.
Uncertain, we light our signal fires and await
whatever whim of the gods will decide our fate—
throwing us capriciously back in the tide,

carelessly dividing, casting this lot aside
while gathering that lot according to a mysterious design
for some use—either probably tortuous or improbably
sublime."

Now, ten years later, the words seemed awkward to her. But the despair she felt, and the fate she'd written of then, was finally playing out today. She'd waited long enough. For ten years. After college she'd taken a job as a translator in a publishing house. She enrolled in a photography class. She'd signed up for group tours, learned to ski, joined "Keep Fit" at the Y, "Great Books" at the library, singles groups at the churches. She'd met people, known them, mostly couples and women, had them for dinner, gone to concerts and plays with them. But always there had been a distance, an awkwardness at some crucial point, something avoided that at last could not be avoided. So there came the drifting, the inevitable loosening, fewer phone calls, schedules that didn't so easily match up. Then the process repeated itself with different faces and names.

She'd become part of the women's movement but was shocked to discover that somehow she'd come to feel less female than just neuter. Her problem wasn't her sex but her mark, her brand. She felt less oppressed than isolated, cut off from men, from women, even from herself. What could be proved when there were no rules for the proving?

She'd even put away all the mirrors in her house. But there were still windows at night, glass in pictures, chrome appliances. And there were still people's eyes, and the inescapable reflections. When everyone went East, she'd gone with them. She tried meditation, but just when she'd relaxed into breathing, and could hear her own heart beat, and emptied her mind, a bloody fingerprint would materialize in her consciousness. Every time. Finally she surrendered to the unavoidable. She'd made a decision, chosen the day. She knew what and how. She stood and moved quickly. The time had come.

She went to the incense box, got fresh sticks, put them in the holders and lit them. The incense would mask the odor. Then she went to the kitchen, blew out all the pilot lights on the stove and then deliberately turned on the gas of each burner and the oven. Back in the living room, she switched on her stereo, put on the record she'd chosen. It was Bach's magnificent B Minor Mass. That was the only music that seemed appropriate to her. Maybe, when they saw what she had played that day, it would help them to understand. Then she laid down on the couch, shut her eyes to wait. The incense smelled lovely to her, blotting out everything else. Except the memories—the color of the great window over the altar, all green and blue and red, and the bells ringing and the chants.

She began to recite from memory, "Let my prayer be counted as incense before thee . . . and the lifting up of my . . . "

She hesitated a moment. Then she went on: " . . . the lifting up of my life as a sacrifice."

She imagined just floating away with the incense. The music was so majestic. Christmas. Christ—mass. Her mass. They had brought him frankincense and gold and myrrh, hadn't they, at his birth. Did they burn the incense in the stable? Blot out the animal smells? Christ—mass. Her mass. Bells and the beautiful priest swinging the great smoking golden censer. She wondered how long it would take and whether she'd smell any gas. Her cat meowed and jumped on her stomach. She sat up with a start.

"Oh my God," she cried. "I forgot all about you, Abelard. I'm sorry. Come on, come on. I'll put you out."

She went to the kitchen door, opened it, put one foot out, kept the other against the door, stooped to put the cat out when suddenly he squirmed and raked her hand with his claw. She jumped, slipped on the ice, caught herself just as the door slammed shut behind her. She was locked out. She shook the door. She pounded on it. She began to cry, frantically, in little sobs.

"Please. Oh please. I can't stand it," she sniffled. She was frantic. And suddenly enraged. She raised her voice: "How can I get in? I have to get in. God help me. Damn it, help me. You . . . You . . . "

She looked around. Maybe the kitchen window was unlatched. She stood on her toes but couldn't reach it. She jumped but couldn't hang on to the sill. She looked for something to stand on.

"The garbage can," she thought to herself. "That's it." She pulled the old metal can over under the window and managed to climb up on it. It was precarious. She tried to hang on with one hand

and push the window up with the other. The can wobbled. She clutched for balance.

"Come on, damn it," she gasped.

"Hey, lady, can I help?" asked a big, male voice.

The voice startled her. She tried to look over her shoulder, clutch at her robe and hang on simultaneously. She whirled in mid-air, the can went out from under her, and she fell in a great somer-sault, landing on her ass, the garbage settling around her. He laughed.

"Bravo!!! Magnificent!"

"What the hell are you laughing at, you stupid idiot?" she screamed at him, not knowing whether to laugh or cry herself. "I could have broken my damn neck. Who the hell are you? What do you want?"

"Hey, I'm sorry," he said, choking back his laughter. "You just looked so funny, flipping ass over tea kettle like that. You hurt? Naw, not swearing like that, you aren't. Much, anyhow. Here, let me help you up." Little spurts of laughter and spray kept escaping his clenched mouth.

"Just leave me alone, thank you. What are you doing back here, anyway. Just go on. Go away. Get out of here."

She stood, clutching her robe, checking for cuts, brushing the garbage off, feeling completely ridiculous.

"Yeah, okay, okay," he shrugged. "Look, I'm the garbage man. I come every Tuesday and Friday. Thought you mighta noticed by now. Got my own truck. Franchised this route. Been doing this part of town for a couple of years. My name is Cohen. Tony Cohen. I'll just gather this garbage here and leave, like you said. But . . . what the hell were you doing on that garbage can, anyway?"

"Trying to get in my house, what do you think?" She tried to sound a little conciliatory.

"Hey, you got locked out? Maybe I can help. You trying to get in that window, huh? Let's see if I can open it for you."

Instantly she regretted her conciliatory tone and put an edge in her voice. "Don't bother. Please. Just take the garbage and go. Just .. go."

"No bother, really."

Before she could protest further, he'd found a foothold, boosted himself up, pushed the window in one quick motion and was back on the ground.

He smiled a crooked smile. "Now if you'll just put your foot in my hand here, I'll boost you up and you can climb right in."

She was torn between embarrassment and panic. Panic prevailed. She had to get back in the house before something else happened. No time for ceremony. Besides, his crooked smile was nice. She did as he said, trying her best to keep her robe securely around her and her nightgown down, and then wondered why it mattered, under the circumstances. She managed to flop her way in the window, across the counter and down onto the floor. The Mass was playing full volume, and the smell of the incense was heavy and pervasive. She looked at the stove and back down at the garbage man.

"Thank you. Thank you very much," she said.

"You're welcome. Very welcome."

"You can go now. I've got to . . . get busy."

"Of course."

He didn't move. He must expect something else. She thought a minute. "I'd like to . . . ah . . . pay you something," she ventured. "Just wait a minute, and I'll get my purse."

"Rather have a cup of coffee, ma'am," he answered.

She moaned to herself and looked at the stove.

It was absurd. Just absurd. She'd planned it all so carefully in her mind, and everything was going wrong.

"You can buy yourself a cup of coffee with the money I'll give you," she countered.

"But I'll have to drink it alone then," he explained with his crooked smile.

She relented. "Oh, all right. Just a minute."

She hurried to the stove and turned off all the gas. Then she went to the door and opened it. He came in.

"What's that smell?" he asked.

"Incense."

"Incense? Sure that's all? Smells awful powerful."

"So do you," she shot back defensively.

"Yeah, I know," he laughed. "I actually stink, you might say. We all do, more or less. You must like incense, though."

She was puzzled. Didn't he know when he'd been insulted? Yet somehow she felt glad he hadn't been offended, which puzzled her even more. She smiled quickly and said, "Yes, I like incense. It helps create a sort of . . . mood, you might say."

"Yeah," he nodded. "I guess it does all right. My mother, she's big on smells."

"She is?"

"Oh yeah," he answered. "Real big. Not incense, though. She probably associates that with cardinals and idols and all that. She's pretty anti-catholic. Actually anti lots of stuff when you come to think of it. Anyway, I was in this church once, downtown. Smelled something like this, you know. But, like I was saying, mother's not much for incense. Just, you know, matches in the bathroom, stuff like that."

"Matches in the bathroom?" asked Jane.

"Oh yeah. You never heard of that? You know, you strike a match, and the sulphur smell and the smoke cover up . . . well, you know . . . the other smells . . . in the bathroom. But matches were more common when I was a kid. Now it's air wick and spray cans of room deodorant and stuff like that. Whole house smells like lily of the valley or whatever the smell of the month is. She's big on smells, my mother. Actually, she's big on covering up smells, is more like it. I guess most people are, you know, big on covering up smells, right? One lady on my route even sprays her plastic garbage bag before she gives it to me. She don't like me being a garbage collector, I can tell you!"

"Who?" laughed Jane. "The lady that sprays her plastic bags?"

"Naw, not that lady. My mother. She wanted me to be a doctor or lawyer or somebody important like that. She couldn't admit that I'm a little slow for that. I almost didn't make it through high school. I wasn't much interested in book learning, I guess." He laughed softly, easily, seemingly at himself. "I got a brother who's a dentist, though. That gives her something to brag about with her friends, you know— her son the dentist. Don't talk much about her son the garbage collector though. But that's all right, don't you think?" He looked at her for agreement. "It's just her, you know?"

She nodded slightly. "I guess."

"My mother makes me take off my garbage clothes in the garage and wear a tie in the house and . . . Hey, I'm boring you."

Actually, she was fascinated. The man was so present, so open, so ingenuous.

"No," she protested. "You're not. Go on, please. Go on Mr. . . . I guess I didn't catch your name."

"Cohen. You can call me Tony, though, if you want. But what about that coffee?"

"Oh. Ah . . . well, ah, the . . . the stove isn't working. I forgot about that."

"Oh yeah? What's wrong?" he asked. "Maybe I can fix it. Let me look."

He'd been standing by the door, hat in hand. He put his hat on the table, crossed to the stove, bent over it. Then slowly he straightened up and looked at her questioningly.

"Smells like a lot of gas over here," he said slowly. "A lot of gas."

"Well, maybe . . . maybe the pilot lights are out. Or something."

He looked at her for a long time before he spoke.

"Yeah," he said. "Or something."

He kept looking at her. There was puzzlement and something close to embarrassment in his eyes. Quietly he crossed back to the table, took his hat in his hand and stood at the open door. She watched him.

"You're going?" she asked.

"I . . . I'm not sure what to say, you know? I feel sort of stupid talking so much like I did. The incense, it was to cover up . . . the gas smell, right? But why? Why would you . . ." his hand pressed his eyes, finishing the question.

She bit her lip and shrugged, looking at her slippers. Then she looked directly at him, engaged his eyes and traced her birthmark with her fingers. He studied her, trying to get his mind focused on what it was she was telling him. He looked at her hand, graceful against the purple mark.

"Yeah," he said, at last. "I was going to ask you about that. It's a birthmark, isn't it? I got a lot of moles on me, you might have noticed."

She hadn't. But now she saw he had a brown mole on the side of his nose, another on his cheek, several small ones on his neck.

He spoke first. "Yours is kind of obvious, I grant you. And ugly, too, to tell the truth. Got you down, huh?"

It was the first time anyone had just matter-of-factly said her birthmark was ugly. She was nonplussed.

"Ugly?" she growled. "Ugly is the best you could say about it. God's bloody fingerprint is what it is. God's bloody damn fingerprint. Can you imagine what it's like to go through life disfigured like this? Can you?"

She fumed and paced. He cracked his knuckles, trying to figure out something. He looked at his hands, then at her, then back at his hands. Finally he said what had come to his mind.

"I think maybe it's something like being a Jew. And being sorta dumb. And a garbage collector."

"A Jew?" she asked. "What are you talking about? I don't get it."

"I mean," replied Tony, "you can't do nothing about it, you know? Some things just are the way they are. You're born with a mark, you got it all your life. Same as me being a Jew. You're born a Jew, you're a Jew. That's that. You get circumcised, right? And isn't that something like God's bloody fingerprint? Sure it is. Thing is, it's supposed to be a mark of being God's chosen people, right? Something special. A covenant forever, right? And what happens? Easy pickings? Milk and honey? Check again! Jews get persecuted all the time, since from the beginning. Kicked around. Hauled into slavery. Shoved into ghettos. Lose their land, everything. Get gassed, burned. My mother, she goes on this trip with some people from the synagogue, right? So they go to this place, Buchenwald, and some lady in the group crawls right up into one of the ovens there, because that's where her sister had died back in 1944; and she wanted to feel for a minute what it must have been like for her sister. See, it's in our blood, like, in the seed we come from. JEW. So this lady gets in the oven and starts crying and won't come out, and finally they had to get a rabbi to come tell her it was okay, to come on out. That it was okay that she hadn't died when her sister did. Took hours to persuade her. Maybe she knew in her blood that everything wasn't okay. Some things, but not everything. Besides, what does okay mean, anyway? It's hard to figure. Talk about God's bloody fingerprint."

He looked out the door to hide his tears. Then he said so softly it was hard to hear, "My Father died at Auschwitz. He managed to help my mother and older brother get out of the country earlier. He was going to come later but . . . She was pregnant with me at the time. Probably that's why she wants me to be . . . somebody, you know?"

She went to the stove and put her head down on it, thinking about what she had planned to do. "O God, I'm sorry, Cohen." They were quiet for a long moment. Then suddenly it struck her.

"Cohen," she said, "if the gas had kept . . . leaking from the stove, would the incense burning have made it explode?"

"Probably. Yeah."

She felt a great surge of relief. She hadn't thought about that, how others might have been hurt. Tears came to her eyes, surprising her. All of a sudden she seemed to care.

"Do you believe in God, Cohen? I mean, do you? It doesn't sound like it . . . from what you were saying about being a Jew and everything. It doesn't seem to matter, about your being chosen and special and all that. Anyway, do you?"

Somehow the question was important to her, terribly important. She wondered why she was asking it, asking this stranger, this garbage collector.

"I didn't say it didn't matter, being a Jew," Tony said. "I just said there were some things you couldn't do anything about. So I'm a man. I'm a Jew. I'm . . . sorta dumb. And God is . . . whatever God is, you know? What is it to believe? That something should work? Get better, be easy? What? I go to the synagogue, and I listen to the rabbi read the Torah, and I try to follow but I don't do too good. I think about other things, sometimes. Who puts the thoughts in my head? I don't know. Anyway, I remember this story I read a long time ago about this clown somewhere who broke his son's legs to make him walk funny."

She gasped. "Oh my God. That's cruel. It didn't really happen, did it? It's inhuman."

"Maybe. But I thought about it for a long time. 'Why would the clown do that?' I asked the rabbi, and all he said was 'Jews are not clowns.' 'But human beings are,' I said. And I asked him, 'What about Ezekiel?' The rabbi got angry. So I shut up. But I kept thinking about that clown. Did he break his son's legs because he didn't love him? Naw, I don't think so. I think it was because . . . because he wanted his son to be a clown, like he was; make people laugh, like he did. So he made it so the son would walk funny, like he did. I mean, I think this clown was crippled himself, only nobody ever asks about that. And laughter, maybe that heals people inside. Maybe you got to feel some pain before you can know what life is and make people really laugh. Maybe that clown wanted to share his life; I mean, really share it with his son, so his son would know from the inside, like. So he did the only thing he knew how to do, so the son would know and stay close to him. And being crippled the son wouldn't have to go to the army and hurt anybody. So what is it to believe in God?"

"And you think it's like that with God?" asked Jane. "Is that it?"

"Who's to say how it is with God?" Tony shrugged. "It's a story about a clown, is all."

"If there is a God, he must be mad."

"What does mad mean?" he asked. "What does okay mean? Maybe it's different than we think. Anyway, I just go on collecting garbage, you know."

"Is it such a bad job?"

"Depends on who you ask," replied Tony. "My mother, she can't think of anything worse. 'Wear a tie,' she says. 'Soak in this oil, spray on that shave lotion. Wash with this soap, that soap, latest thing.' Sorry, I still stink. But you know, so does everybody else. So everybody's got garbage. Everybody's got bathroom smells. You try to disguise, cover up, deny it. It's still there. Garbage—you can either disguise it and dump it on somebody else, or pick it up and deal with it. Seems to me better to collect it than to hide it. So being a garbage man helps keep me honest, you know. Reminds me of things. Like God's bloody fingerprints. So don't be so proud. You aren't the only one. Yours is just more obvious. Got to deal with it. You know the

Jewish legend of the Just Men?"

"No."

"Well, it's that God's supposed to keep always a few Just Men on earth . . . women, too, I suppose. Anyway, they don't always know they are the Just Men, and most other people, they don't know either. But without these Just Men, the world would choke on its own garbage, so to speak. The Just Men . . . or Women . . . they suffer a lot, feel a lot of pain, have their hearts broken. But they laugh and sing a lot, too. And because they live, the world lives. And God is close to them, even though they don't know it. I mean, they don't feel it so much. There's something about it in the Bible. In Isaiah. I read it every once in awhile. You'd like it."

"I would?" Jane asked.

"Sure. You get a Bible, and I'll light those pilots, and we'll have some coffee and I'll read it to you."

So it happened. The Bible was found, the coffee made. She watched him sipping coffee and leafing slowly through the book, and something in her was deeply glad and at ease.

"Okay, here it is," said Tony. "Now listen."

He read slowly, deliberately, as a child would: " *'Who has believed what we have heard? And to whom has the arm of the Lord been revealed? For he grew up before him like a young plant, and like a root out of the dry ground; he had no form or comeliness that we should look at him, and no beauty that we should desire him . . .'* "

As he read, she began to weep, great tears rolling down her cheeks, washing over God's bloody fingerprint, splashing on the table. He continued: " *'All we like sheep have gone astray; We have turned every one to his own way; And the Lord has laid on him the iniquity of us all.'* There. That's how it is for the Just Men. And Just Women. Hey, you're crying."

She nodded and then began to sob aloud. He touched her hand, softly. She took his hand in both of hers, felt its roughness.

"It's a hard life, sometimes," he spoke gently. "But it's what we've got. God's bloody fingerprint?"

He looked at her, questioningly, waiting. She looked back, shuddering at the end of her tears.

"At least it's . . . God's fingerprint . . . bloody or not. It's okay, Cohen! Thanks!"

He reached over and touched her birthmark, tenderly, tracing it with his finger. No one, except doctors, had ever touched it before, and no one ever like that.

"I'd like to come back tonight, after work," he said.

She nodded.

"If you keep the gas off, I'll take a long bath. Agree?"

She smiled. And so did he.

"And not too much incense. I won't smell that bad."

"It doesn't matter how you smell, Stinky," she replied.

"And it doesn't matter how you look, Ugly."

They laughed. Then they were shy. He dropped his hat, picked it up, and bumped into the door on his way out. He almost forgot her garbage, but then he remembered and scooped it into his big container and backed around the corner of the house.

She watched him and lifted a hand to wave, and when he had gone she put her hand to her cheek. She felt very alive, oddly graceful. For the first time she allowed herself to believe that under God's bloody fingerprint there just might be a strange, wondrous world to explore.

That night when Cohen came back, there was a single candle in the window, a single stick of incense in the corner of the room, and a wordless sort of prayer in her heart. As the night wore on, you could hear laughter in that house. And with the incense you could smell hope. And under the birthmark you could see, like the pulse of life itself, the throb of love.

"And there will be signs in the sun and moon and stars, and upon the earth distress . . . Now when these things begin to take place, look up and raise your heads, because your redemption is drawing near." *

---

*Luke 21: 25, 28, RSV

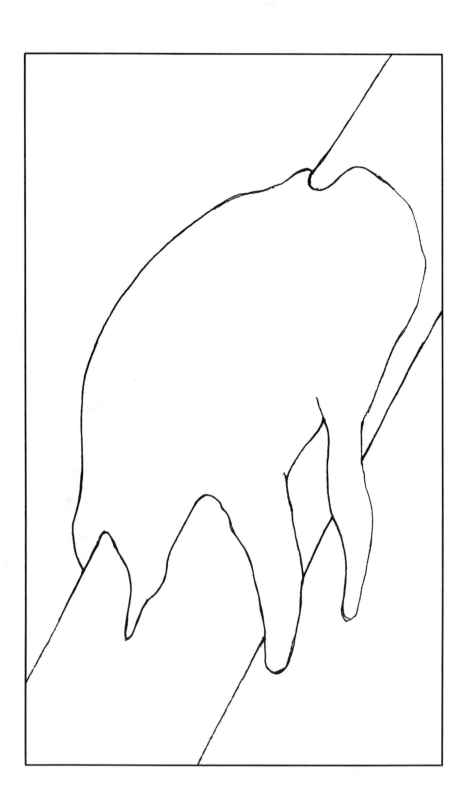

Gum on the Altar

W hen the chariots of the Lord, rolling out on shafts of light and through timeless darknesses and unknown worlds, break rank to wheel and scatter round planets like our own, finding their way into curious and unlikely corners of such planets—for curious and unlikely reasons, bearing curious and unlikely messages—you might guess there are curious and unlikely creatures in them, hanging on to the reins as much to stay in the chariot as to guide it. Who knows where such messages, and messengers, might end up? So it is well to pay attention!

Consider, if you will, two old women walking to lunch, as snow begins to fall. Could they be . . .?

"It's snowing, Rose," observed one of the women named Phoebe.

Rose, the other woman, engaged in what are truly her own thoughts, mumbled to herself, "Do you think green would match the trees if I opened the door to sneeze when the gardener squeezed and the air is nice if it's blue as ice but Mrs. Vassick ain't so full of spice and . . ."

"Rose. ROSE!"

"Yes? Oh, Phoebe, it's you. Yes it is. Yes. What?"

"It's snowing, Rose."

"Well, yes it is," Rose agreed. "It certainly is. Yes, it is. It is snowing. Yes, certainly, it is. It is . . ."

"Rose!"

"Yes? Yes, Phoebe?"

"Rose, I heard no two snowflakes is alike. Not one like another."

"Is that a fact?" exclaimed Rose. "Well now, ain't that something. Just imagine that. Ain't no two snowflakes alike. Ain't that something. Think of . . . How did they find that out, Phoebe?"

"I don't know. I just heard it's so."

"My. Now, ain't they getting smart," said Rose. "They just know everything these days, don't they. Imagine knowing ain't no two snowflakes alike. Imagine knowing these snowflakes we're mashing under our feet right now ain't like no other snowflakes anywhere forever and ever. How do they know that, Phoebe? That no snowflakes ain't like no other snowflakes forever and ever and never and lever and river and . . ."

"Rose."

"Yes?"

"Rose, how many snowflakes do you think there are?"

"Well, let me see," Rose answered. "A lot! Certainly a lot. Oh, a very lot. A thousand, probably. Oh, more. More than a thousand. A hundred thousand? A thousand thousand? Oh, I know it's a very, very lot. How many, Phoebe?"

"Zillions, Rose. Zillions and trillions and millions."

"Is that a fact, Phoebe? That many. Well, now ain't that something. That is something, ain't it? That certainly is a lot. A very, very lot. A very, very, very . . . "

"Rose!"

"Yes? Yes, Phoebe. Yes. What is it?"

"Who makes snowflakes?" asked Phoebe.

"Who makes snowflakes? Oh, well now . . . let me see. Who makes snowflakes? Who makes . . . let me see. I . . . ah . . . I don't know, Phoebe. I don't know, do I, Phoebe? I should know, but I forgot. I'm going to cry. I am. Going to cry. I don't know. I just forgot."

"Rose! Don't cry, Rose. It's all right. I'll tell you who makes snowflakes. God makes snowflakes, that's who."

"Oh, good for you, Phoebe! You remembered. Good for you. Of course. God makes snowflakes, I forgot. Ain't that something? Of course. Certainly God makes . . . How do they know that, Phoebe?"

"Reverend Thurston says so, in chapel," answered Phoebe. "He says that God makes everything. Remember?"

"Did he say that? Oh, yes. Of course, he did. I remember now. Ain't that something. God makes everything. Snowflakes, too. Certainly, of course."

"Besides," confided Phoebe, "last night I heard little voices and they kept saying, 'God made us, God made us.' Over and over. And I looked all around, and it was the snowflakes talking through the window. Did you hear 'em?"

But Rose was off in her own thoughts again, talking to herself. "Coke is good. I like coke, and I don't smoke or tell no jokes and old cow pokes and . . . why don't they let me have cokes? Is two small cokes more than one big coke? I asked the man, but he said I didn't have enough money. Two cents, I had. Change. Home on the range. Where everything's strange . . . "

"ROSE! Listen to me, Rose."

"Oh, Phoebe? It's you. Yes. Certainly. I was listening. Yes, I certainly was. I was, yes, I was, and . . . and you was talking about . . . about . . . "

"Snowflakes, Rose."

"Yes. That was it. Good for you, Phoebe! You remembered. Good for you. That was it. We was talking about snowflakes. Of course. Certainly. Phoebe, you look sort of sick. What's the matter, dear?"

"Rose, I ain't sick. Now just shut up a minute. I'm just thinking, is all. Rose, if God makes snowflakes, and no two snowflakes is alike, and there are zillions and trillions of snowflakes, God must be terrible busy. So how does God have time to do much else but make snowflakes?"

"How does He have time to do . . . oh my," Rose struggled. "That's a hard one. Let me see. I should know the answer to that, shouldn't I? Let me see . . . Maybe snowflakes . . . Maybe snowflakes . . . Maybe God . . . I can't remember. I'm going to cry, Phoebe. I'm just going to cry."

"Don't cry, Rose. It's all right. Maybe they'll let you have a coke for lunch."

Two women, curious and unlikely creatures, on their way to lunch as the snow falls in a curious and unlikely corner of the planet—The State Mental Hospital—where they are for curious and unlikely reasons, though perhaps no more curious and unlikely than any of us curious and unlikely creatures are wherever it is that we are.

The last of the many jobs Phoebe did to support her invalid mother was as a street vendor of hot dogs and soda. Her cart was mounted on a three-wheel bicycle she rode about town. When her mother died, Phoebe kept riding her cart, selling her hot dogs and listening to the voices she'd begun to hear about a year before.

One evening she'd ridden her cart to a corner near the Opera House where stylishly dressed people had to walk around her while she hawked her wares. When a policeman told her to move, she argued that she wouldn't, because stronger voices than his had told her to come to that particular corner on that particular night, and she wouldn't move, "Thank you very much, get lost Buddy Boy!" The argument got heated, the policeman threatened to arrest her, and Phoebe began throwing paper cups and hot dog wrappers—and then the hot dogs and buns—around on the sidewalk, and a crowd gathered. When the embarrassed policeman took Phoebe by the arm to lead her away, she'd kicked him and thrown soda on his uniform. He called a wagon and they'd picked her up bodily and carted her away.

After a night in jail, the court committed Phoebe to The State Mental Hospital for psychiatric tests. The tests were legally inconclusive, but since she had no family or outside advocate, her case got conveniently buried. So the women's geriatric ward became home for Phoebe.

Rose had been married. Her one child, a son, had run off to join the Merchant Marine at seventeen and had not been heard from again. Rose's heart was broken. After her husband died, she'd ended up living alone in a small apartment on his pension. At first she had a cat to talk to, but after a while she'd begun talking not only to the cat but to herself. Slowly she seemed to lose track of things, including the thread of her own conversations.

Then one winter evening, a policeman had found her shivering on a street corner talking rapidly in what seemed to him an irrational and incoherent way. They'd detained her in the Women's Detention Center for several weeks, but tracing her through missing persons turned up nothing and Rose simply couldn't remember where she lived or anyone she knew. So after much indecision, someone in the Welfare Department suggested The State Mental Hospital and, thus nudged into the bureaucratic maze, Rose found her way at last to the women's geriatric ward and the bed next to Phoebe's.

So Phoebe and Rose had become inseparable. One was round, the other bony. One shuffled along, the other swayed in a bow-legged way. One talked to herself, the other heard voices. Neither could put into words how they felt about the other, and it did not occur to them to try. They didn't even think about it. They were simply inseparable.

"Here's the dining room, Rose," said Phoebe. "Give me your arm for the steps."

"Orange is nice, all sticky and spice, icky as mice, ran up the clock, hickory dock, cat on the block, which one is right, right is nice, nice is bright, bright is nice, nice is . . . . " Rose rambled on.

"Rose."

"Yes? Oh, Phoebe. It's you. I was listening, I certainly was. Certainly, yes, listening I was. I was, really, I . . ."

"Here is the dining room," instructed Phoebe. "Give me your arm for the steps."

"Oh yes! Good, good, good. Time for lunch. Thanks a bunch.

Do you think I can have a coke? Phoebe, do you think I can have a coke? For lunch? Do you? Do you think I can, do you, do you, do you?"

"Maybe," replied Phoebe. "Maybe you can have a coke, and I can get some gum. Got a quarter in my pocket. For the gum machine. Pull the lever; it says, 'Thank you!' Do you hear it say that, Rose? Pull the lever; it says, 'Thank you. Here comes the gum. Thank you! Thank you!' Do you hear it, Rose?"

One loved coke, the other loved gum. Curious and unlikely! Though Phoebe didn't have many teeth left, she loved to chew gum, though chewing was only one thing she did with gum —perhaps the least of the things she did with it. She sucked on it, gummed it, rolled it around in her mouth, swallowed it, blew bubbles with it (if it was bubble gum, getting it all over her face), pulled it out of her mouth in long strings, put it behind her ear sometimes where it usually got stuck in her hair.

Worst of all, she would leave wads of chewed gum everyplace. Many of the places she left it, and forgot about it, were harmless enough. Often she would leave it on her little bed stand overnight and chew it again the next day, marveling at how hard it got during the night, and how she could see her tooth marks in it just as she'd left it when she'd gone to bed. But other places she left her gum were more troublesome. Phoebe and Rose worked in the hospital laundry together, Rose folding towels, Phoebe folding sheets. Many times Phoebe had left her used gum next to a pile of just-washed sheets before they were rolled through the big mangle irons. Often her gum ended up sticking on the sheets when they were rolled through the mangles, and the resulting mess caused furor after furor until finally the laundry supervisor simply forbid her to chew gum which, for the most part, she didn't while she worked.

Still, her gum also caused problems when she accidently left it where people sat, or walked. To top everything, when Reverend Thurston came, once a month, to give Holy Communion in the chapel over the dining room in her building, Phoebe would invariably go forward with the others to receive the elements, only to remember her gum just as the bread was being passed. So, just as invariably, she would remove her gum and put it, only for a moment she thought, on the communion rail while she chewed the bread, thinking it would be terrible to mix her chewing gum with the "Body of Christ." And, invariably, she forgot about her gum and left it behind when she returned to her pew. So, regularly, Reverend Thurston stopped by in the ward on his way back to his church and gave her a little talk about good manners in worship, which meant, specifically, that she should not chew gum in the chapel. She was never sure exactly what he was saying, or why, but each time, she agreed not to chew during worship, only to forget her agreement by the time the next month's communion had come around.

Recently, Reverend Thurston had approached her again about the gum she'd left on the rail during the Advent communion service.

"Phoebe," Reverend Thurston had admonished, "you put your gum on the communion rail again. You simply must stop doing that. It is irreverent, it is offensive to God and it desecrates a holy place."

"I'm sorry, Reverend," Phoebe answered. "I just forget. I don't mean no harm, really. What does des-e-crate mean?"

"It means . . . well . . ." Thurston groped for words to explain what it never occurred to him needed explaining. "It means to take something clean and make it dirty. Phoebe, how would you like it if someone took your clean sheets and got them all dirty after you washed and folded them? Well, that's how God feels about gum on the communion rail."

"But, Reverend, ain't people supposed to get sheets dirty? If you use 'em, how can you keep from getting 'em dirty? That's why we wash 'em. I don't understand about des-e-crate."

"Well," stammered Thurston, feeling flustered, "desecrate is, well . . . it's . . . it's taking something that's supposed to be used one way, the right way, and using it another way, the wrong way. That's what desecrate means. Using something wrongly, for what it wasn't intended to be used for. You see what I mean, Phoebe?" He felt pleased with himself.

"I think so," Phoebe nodded, smiling. "It's like Jesus being born in a stable, like you read in the Bible to us. That's using the stable for another way than was meant, right? Jesus desecrated the stable.

Is that sorta what you mean?"

"No, that is not at all what I mean." Thurston's face contorted between anger and foolishness. "Phoebe, you are deliberately refusing to see my point."

"I ain't trying to miss it, Reverend. Really. I'll . . . I'll remember next time not to chew gum. Don't worry, Reverend."

"Good." Thurston was relieved to leave the subject of desecration. "Just think how other people feel, seeing your gum on the rail when they come to the Lord's Table, Phoebe. Try to remember next time." He turned to leave.

"Excuse me, Reverend, but . . . I been wondering about them wisemen, you know, the ones you read about? Why did they bring them gifts to baby Jesus?"

"To honor him as King and Diety," answered Reverend Thurston, turning back.

"But what is franka . . . franka . . . "

"Frankincense, Phoebe? It is like incense. It smells good. It's used to worship the Diety. It means Jesus is Lord."

"Oh. And what about the other stuff they brung? Not the gold. The other stuff. You know."

"Yes, myrrh. That is like a rare resin, Phoebe."

"Resin? What's that?"

"Well, it's like a kind of gummy substance," replied Reverend Thurston.

Phoebe brightened. "Gummy? Like gum?"

"Not gum gum, Phoebe. It's more like . . . well, they use it to make perfume and to make a liquid they used to bury people with in ancient times."

"Oh. Bury people. Ain't that a stupid thing to bring a little baby, Reverend?"

"It's symbolic, Phoebe. They brought it because they knew Jesus would die for the sins of the world. As it says in the Bible, in Revelation, 'Worthy is the Lamb who was slain, to receive power and wealth and wisdom and might and honor and glory and blessing.' It's symbolic, the myrrh."

"A lamb, Reverend? I don't get it."

"Well, Phoebe, that's symbolic, too. A lamb is a symbol of

innocence, you see. A little lamb is innocent. And Jesus was innocent. An innocent sacrifice is acceptable to God. Because of it, God forgives our sins."

"Sort of like Jesus helps us and helps God," Phoebe mused.

"In a manner of speaking," Thurston replied.

"And that's what myrrh means?" she asked.

"That is what it means. Or close enough for you. Now, I have to go. Just remember, Phoebe, no more gum in the chapel." He sighed as he walked away.

Phoebe didn't understand what Reverend Thurston was saying, but probably he didn't either, though his departing sigh was as close as he'd ever come to admitting it, even to himself. So the difference was that she was troubled by not understanding and he wasn't. She struggled to understand, because she knew she didn't; and he didn't struggle to understand, because he thought he did. And that is how messages get missed—curious and unlikely messages from curious and unlikely creatures hanging on for dear life to the reins of the Lord's chariot wheeling in curious and unlikely places.

The dining room of Phoebe's and Rose's unit was on the first floor in the center of a two-story building. The chapel was over the dining room on the second floor, so, "symbolically," God and the kitchen held together the women's geriatric ward in the east wing and the men's geriatric ward in the west wing. It was an old building, built before electricity or inside plumbing or central heating. So when each of these conveniences was added, all sorts of conduits and pipes were attached to the walls. When you entered the building, you felt a little like Jonah in the belly of the whale, watching and listening to its vital juices pass through its tracts and ducts and glands. Rumor had it that the old building was to be torn down soon and another built to replace it.

So it was into the belly of this whale that Rose and Phoebe entered. They made their way to their table and had just sat down when Dr. Kaplan announced that the Trinity Church youth choir would be singing Christmas carols for them that noon, and the auxiliary of the local Rotary Club would pass out gifts. The gifts turned out to be a box of Kleenex and a bag of candy for everyone. Phoebe gladly noted that the bag of candy had a package of gum in it. Suddenly overwhelmed by the prospect, she began to cry.

And no sooner than the choir began to sing, Rose began to talk: "Trick or treat, kiss my feet. Wear your rubbers, oh yes, mother. Bundle up, you'll catch your death, look at there, you can see your breath. Johnny's all dead and gone. Everybody sing a song. Red is dead and so's the brain inside your head, and so is Fred with dirty feet . . . "

"Rose, shhh," whispered Phoebe, "they're singing."

Rose blithely babbled on, "Freddy stinks and Mary winks and Daddy drinks. But I won't tell so what the hell . . . "

"Rose, Rose, shhh. They're singing. SHHHHHHHHH. ROSE."

"Yes? Oh, Phoebe. It's you. I was listening. Really. I was . . . Oh, Phoebe, you're crying. Oh, don't cry. Please, don't cry. What's the matter? Oh, I'm going to cry, too. Oh, Phoebe, Phoebe."

"Shhh, Rose. I'm just feeling a little bad 'cause people give us things, and I ain't got nothing to give nobody. Not even you, Rose. Nothing to give for Christmas."

"Ahh, Phoebe, you're my friend. You give me you. Best thing anybody could have. You're my friend. Don't feel bad, please. You're the nicest friend anybody ever had. Don't cry, Phoebe, please don't."

"Shhhh. Rose, be quiet. Listen to the music now. Stop talking and listen. Shhhh."

Rose turned to listen and Phoebe looked at her a long time, thinking about what she had said, until the choir finished and everyone was clapping. An idea had begun to form in her mind.

Another curious thing about this curious place was that many of the buildings of The State Mental Hospital were connected by underground tunnels which were used for walkways as well as passages for plumbing and heating lines. In fact, much of the life of the hospital took place in those tunnels and in the veritable warren of storage rooms and closets running off them. Since the snow continued to fall, Phoebe and Rose and most of the other patients used the tunnels to return to their afternoon activities.

On their way back, the group stopped and gathered in a large storage room where several mattresses had been put on the floor and an old record player stood in one corner. At odd hours, especially at night, patients would sneak down to this room for little parties and social liasons, all officially forbidden but unofficially sanctioned by the hospital authorities. Such activities obviously helped patient morale and so helped the hospital run more smoothly. And on this particular day, many in the little gathering were grumbling about the gift of Kleenex and wishing some group would give them some beer sometime, or something for a party.

But while they grumbled, Phoebe was busy trading her candy to women for their gum and giving kisses and other small favors, along with the promises of future considerations, for the men's gum. By the time she returned to the laundry, she had 87 packages of gum and promises of at least 23 more. That night she counted her little savings, slowly dividing it into little piles, each of which would buy a package of gum; she determined she'd be able to buy another 34 packages, maybe more.

During the following week, though no one really noticed, Phoebe left no wads of chewing gum anywhere. And every night, late into the night, Phoebe sat on the edge of her bed chewing stick after stick of gum until her jaws ached.

"Phoebe, what are you doing?" asked Rose sleepily on her midnight return from the bathroom.

"Chewing gum, can't you see?" Phoebe sighed. "Just go to sleep, Rose. Don't worry."

"Why are you chewing all your gum like that, Phoebe? Why don't you save it. You're using it all up. Why are you doing that?"

"I'm making something is why. For Christmas."

"What, Phoebe? What are you making? Something for me? For me, Phoebe? For me?"

"Not exactly for you, Rose. It's a . . . surprise. It's mainly for God."

"God? You're making something for God? Ain't that something. For God. That's something, Phoebe. It certainly is. It is, certainly. How did you know what God wants, Phoebe?"

"I don't know. I just . . . I don't know."

"Surprise. For God. Ain't that something. Phoebe, you said that God made snowflakes, but I forgot what else you said. About snowflakes. What'd you say?"

"That I heard 'em talking?" answered Phoebe.

"That's it. Good for you, Phoebe! You remembered. That's what you said, all right. You heard 'em talking. You certainly did. How come I don't hear 'em, Phoebe?"

"You're too busy talking," Phoebe replied.

"Oh. I never thought of that. What do they say, Phoebe? The snowflakes. What do they say?"

" 'God made us. God made us.' That's what they say, Rose. And Rose, no two snowflakes is alike, remember?"

"That's right," said Rose. "That's what you said. I remember now. And you said there was zillions and zillions of 'em. See, I was listening, Phoebe. I was. How many is a zillion, Phoebe?"

"A lot," Phoebe answered. "A very, very lot, as you say."

"Oh. Why was we talking about that, Phoebe?"

" 'Cause I was wondering, if God made all them snowflakes, how does God have time to do anything else? Answer me that, Rose."

"Oh. OHHHHH. I forgot what you said. Let me see . . . I forgot. I . . . I think I'm going to cry. Phoebe. Yes, I am. I'm going to cry."

"It's all right, Rose. Don't cry. I don't know either. God must be pretty busy. So . . . so I'm making God a little surprise. Now go to sleep."

During that week, Phoebe chewed 137 packages of gum. She used all the money she had saved to buy more, and she begged from doctors and nurses and attendants, and traded with other patients, and even took some from the commissary when the clerk wasn't looking. And every night she chewed. By the week before Christmas she had asked Rose to help her.

"But I don't like to chew gum, Phoebe," said Rose. "I just ain't got no good teeth."

"You gotta help, Rose. Or I won't finish my surprise in time for Christmas."

"But I can't talk good when I chew gum. The gum sticks to my teeth. See, ah caahhn't tahhk gahhd."

"You don't have to talk," said Phoebe. "Just chew and chew and chew, Rose. Rose? Rose did you hear something just then?"

"Ahhh, naaw. Ahh dahhn't heaah nahhthin."

"Shhh. Listen. It's singing, Rose. Singing. You hear it?"

"Naaw, nahhthing. Ahh daahhn't heaah nahh sahhing."

"Chew, Rose. Chew faster. The angels is coming. Already. Listen. That's them singing. Oh, hurry up. Hurry."

So the night before Christmas Eve, Rose and Phoebe sat on their beds across from each other and chewed the last packages of Phoebe's hoard of gum. When they had finished, they gathered the fresh wads of chewed gum, snuck out past the night attendant who was asleep in the little glass enclosed office, and went down stairs into the basement. They made their way along the dimly lit tunnel to a small closet off one of the storage rooms. Phoebe lit a candle she had hidden there.

"See, Rose. That's what I been making," said Phoebe. "That's where the gum I been chewing went. See. What do you think?"

"Why, that's the biggest wad of chewed up gum I ever seen, Phoebe. Ain't that something. It certainly is. It certainly is something, ain't it? You been making that. It's something. What is it, Phoebe?"

"It's a statue, Rose, can't you tell? Here, I'll pick it up so you can see. See, the gum got all hard when I stuck it together. Now, what do you think?"

"Let me see," answered Rose, "I should know what that is. It's . . . it's chewing gum, that's a fact, ain't it? Chewing gum all chewed up, little clumps stuck together in a statue of . . . of . . . of . . . a cat? That's it. A cat! It's a cat is what it is. Like my cat. Emily cat. Nice cat. Orange cat. Orange peal, real meal, happy deal . . . "

"Rose. ROSE!"

"Yes, Phoebe?"

"It is not no cat," said Phoebe. "It is a lamb. Can't you see the wool? Curly all over it. Now, this gum we chewed tonight is for one ear and a little tail. Stick some on right there, and . . . there. Like that. Squeeze it a little. There. Good. That will be hard in the morning. And see there, his legs bent under him, 'cause he's lying down. And this here's the nose. Could of been a little longer, maybe, but I run outta gum. It's a lamb, Rose."

"Good for you, Phoebe! You knew right off it was a lamb. Of course. It certainly is. That's what it is. A lamb. Yes, that's what it is, all right. What are you going to do with it, Phoebe?"

"Put it on the altar. In the chapel. For God."

"Does God chew gum, Phoebe? How did you know that? I didn't know that. Now ain't that something. Certainly is. It certainly is something that you knew . . ."

"NOT TO CHEW, ROSE! It's like, how did Reverend say it, it's symbotic. That's it. Symbotic. Gum is what I love. So this lamb is symbotic of me, of my love. So it'll be like me, on the altar. You see, Jesus was symbotic, like, of the lamb. Or the lamb was symbotic. I ain't too clear on that. But I just thought, since God's got so much to do, with the snowflakes and everything, and . . . I ain't got much but . . . to cheer God up and help out I'd give this . . . symbotic . . . gum lamb . . . of my love . . . or something like that."

Befuddled, Rose returned to her own thoughts and conversation. "Coke is good. Are two small cokes more than one big one? But too much ice is not too nice. Slip on ice, slide on snow. Go and blow and stop the show."

"Rose!"

"Phoebe? It is you. I was listening. I was. I certainly was. I just got thirsty is what happened. Can we get a coke, please. Can we? Please."

"Rose. Rose. Dear Rose. Come on. I got a quarter. We'll sneak down to the dining room machine."

Sneak? No! One shuffled, the other swayed through the tunnel of The State Mental Hospital to the coke machine in the dining room, then back to the women's geriatric ward and bed. Curious unlikely creatures in a curious unlikely place for curious unlikely reasons.

Then it was Christmas Eve, that holiest of times. After the lights were out, Phoebe and Rose snuck out again, easier this time since most of the attendants were off. Down they went to the basement, into the tunnel, on to the little closet where Phoebe picked up her chewing gum lamb which, crude though it was, bore a striking resemblance to a real lamb, since the wads of gum did look surprisingly like tufts of wool. Then slowly the two friends made their way to the dining room and on up to the chapel above.

The chapel was plain, the floor wooden and creaky. The big windows were of clear glass through which, this night, came the soft light of a full moon. The pulpit was on one side of the small platform, the lectern on the other, as Thurston had "properly" arranged them. The altar was on the wall to the rear, and on it were two candles and a cross. A dark curtain ran half way up the wall, and a tiny window, much like a porthole, or a cyclopsian eye, was near the top. The pews sagged, which gave them a tired look, and there was a musty smell about the place. And it was very warm, warmer even than it usually is in a state building for old people. The two women stood timidly at the back, near the door.

"Shhh," whispered Phoebe.

"Shhh?" asked Rose. "Why? Somebody sleeping in here?"

"No. Ain't no service now. Just don't want nobody to hear us."

"Why? What are you going to do, Phoebe?" asked Rose.

"I ain't exactly sure. Say something, Rose. Something religious. You know. Anything."

"Religious? Something religious. Let me see. I should know something. I . . . Oh, yes. 'The Lord is my shepherd. I shall not . . . not . . . ahh . . . shall not. . . ' "

"Want, Rose. Want."

"Want what, Phoebe? What?"

"Nothing, Rose. Just, I shall not want. Want is what you couldn't think of. 'The Lord is my shepherd, I shall not want.' "

"Don't be cross, Phoebe. I just forgot. I forgot. I . . . I'm going to cry. I don't think I like it in here alone like this."

"You ain't alone, Rose. I'm here. Now come on! I'll just put my lamb on the altar and we'll go. Come on."

"Phoebe, I don't like sneaking around like this. Don't like sneaking. Don't like creaking. Yellow's bad but black is sad and green is seen beneath the dream . . . "

"Shhh, Rose! Do you hear something?"

". . . beyond the scheme, the trees are bare, there's no cat hair, the night is spare, there is nowhere . . . "

"Rose! ROSE!"

"Yes? Oh, Phoebe. Yes, I'm listening. I am. I certainly am."

"Do you hear something, Rose? Do you? High, like music?"

"Do I hear . . . music? Do you? What is it, Phoebe? Why can't I hear it?"

"Listen. Listen. Where is it? Voices. Where are they coming from? Where? Where? Come on, Rose. We got to follow 'em. Come on."

They left the chapel and stood in the hallway, listening. To their left were the big wooden doors leading to the women's ward, second floor, and to their right, the same kind of doors leading to the second floor of the men's ward. Those doors were kept locked and looked formidable. But from behind the doors on the men's side came the sound of voices, weak but panicked voices, moans and screams without much volume, as from old men, sick, tired, confused. What looked like smoke was coming from under the doors.

"Look, Phoebe. Look. Look," cried Rose.

"I see. I see. Come on. Quick, quick."

As fast as they could, they moved down the hall and began pushing on the doors.

"Push, Rose. Push. Push," yelled Phoebe. "As hard as you can. Push."

"I am. I am, Phoebe. As hard as I can."

Big as the doors looked, they were old and had been ignored for years. Their locks were old-fashioned, too, and gave way rather easily. The women pushed into the men's ward. It was full of steam—hot, live steam which made it hard to see and harder to breathe. Side gates were up on most beds, and many men were unable to get out of them without help. They were gasping, coughing. Those closest to the leaking steam pipe were being scalded as the steam gushed out from the pipe where it ran along the wall two or three feet off the floor. The pipes were unusually large, because they not only carried steam for the entire wing, but also went from the heating plant, through this building, down into the tunnel and on to three more buildings.

"We got to help these men get out, Rose," shouted Phoebe. "Through the doors. Quick, quick."

Somehow Rose and Phoebe were rejuvenated rather than panicked by the crisis. Coughing, they edged into the room, reaching the first men.

"I can't . . . see too good . . . Phoebe," Rose sputtered, reaching to take one of the old men's hands, then saying to him, "Here, this way . . . this way. Come on . . . that's it. Climb out . . . over the end. Never mind those bars . . . Come on . . . Phoebe . . . Phoebe, where are you?"

Phoebe was crawling along, pushing her lamb ahead of her and toward the hissing sound, following it to its source. The steam hissed and roared, tore at her lungs, clawed at her face, scalded her flesh, and seared her eyes whenever she opened them. Finally, she stood, held her gum lamb in front of her and pushed it with all of her strength at the hissing sound. Slowly the sound muffled. She pushed harder. The steam dissipated slightly. With her hands she could feel where the joint had pulled loose. The heat softened the gum. As best she could, she stuffed it around the leaking wound in the pipe.

Then she turned to help the man in the nearest bed. He was moaning. She tried to push the bed down the aisle toward the door. She couldn't see very well. Her eyes were swollen nearly shut. The pain came with a roar and then a yawning silence. She fell into a merciful blackness.

The next thing she knew, she was lying on her back and someone was holding something to her face, telling her to breathe. It hurt to breathe. She squinted into the light. Rose was holding her hand and crying, "Oh, Phoebe. Oh, Phoebe."

Phoebe could hear something way off. Was it a siren? Or music? She lifted her head, listening. A voice spoke: "Easy. Just take it easy."

She peered as best she could through her swollen lids and could just make out that she was in the chapel, up near the altar. People were moving around. They were all in white, like angels. Other people were lying in the nearby pews.

Bending over her she could see another person in white, looking at her with a bright light, talking in a deep voice to someone she couldn't see: "Some pretty bad burns here. Luckily, everyone got out alive. This woman is the worst. She's burned pretty bad. The word is that she helped save the others. I don't know what she used, but apparently she managed to stop the steam long enough for everyone to get out."

Phoebe pushed the oxygen mask away. She spoke hoarsely, "It was my gum lamb."

"Take it easy, ma'am," the voice said tenderly. Then to the unseen person, it asked more loudly, "What did she say?"

Another voice replied, "I didn't catch it."

"Her gum lamb," replied Rose. "That's what she done. Put her gum lamb on that busted pipe. Ain't that something? Oh, Phoebe. You got to be all right. You got to be. You hear me? You will be, won't you?"

Phoebe smiled and nodded. She had given what was "symbotic" of her love where it was needed. She didn't understand it all, but she was pretty sure God would. In spite of what the Reverend had said to her, she believed what she'd done was a desecration, sort of like the baby Jesus in the stable. Like it, but different. Like snowflakes are alike, but different. She'd helped a little. She lifted her head again, and listened.

"Do you hear something, Rose," she rasped. "That music, do you hear it?"

"Music? Well . . . maybe I do. Yes, I think I do, Phoebe. Ain't that something? I do. I certainly do. I hear it, Phoebe. Really I do. I do hear it."

Ah yes, that music, do you hear it? Before you answer, gentle reader, you will do well to remember who really asks. For when the chariots of the Lord roll out on shafts of light and through timeless darkness and break rank to wheel around planets such as our own, finding their way to curious and unlikely corners of it, for curious and unlikely reasons, bearing curious and unlikely messages embodied in curious and unlikely creatures such as . . . well, who knows? Things are wilder by far than we think and more wondrous than we may yet have dared to believe. So . . . do you hear the music?

"For you shall go out in joy
and be led forth in peace;
the mountains and the hills before you
shall break forth into singing,
and all the trees of the field shall clap their hands." *

---

*Isaiah 55:12, RSV

Epilogue

Nostalgia is a common feeling around religious holidays such as Christmas. It is a common feeling, but at once curious and complicated. Among other things, I suspect it involves a wish that we might have some experiences similar to those associated with the event we're celebrating. If only we could have some angel visitation to instruct or reassure or just persuade us. When we try to conjure it up with costumes and creches, the nostalgia is more emphasized than satisfied, and the disappointment borders on depression.

Part of the problem may be that we really assume that such visitations—such miracles—are quite impossible, and probably always have been, even in those supposedly more primitive and un-enlightened days recorded in the Bible. We assume that those ancients were simply over superstitious and under educated. So they misinterpreted things, or just made them up to help domesticate their world.

But I wonder if our sophistication, our technological advances, haven't so conditioned our perceptual and mental sets that we miss what the ancients actually *did* see and hear in some ways more direct, simple and possibly terrifying than we allow ourselves to experience. Perhaps it is we who have tried to domesticate our world but in that process have only managed to shrink it and make it essentially one-dimensional. And yet . . .

Perhaps Christmas calls our attention, if fleetingly, to another dimension of life, one our "child" believes but our "adult" denies because it would disturb the neatness of our one-dimensional view. We seem to forget that neatness never matters much to a wondering child, or satisfies for long the longing adult who envies the child's wonder.

That other dimension to life is suggested by some graffiti I once came across in the men's room of a Chinese restaurant. Why it was there, and who scrawled it alongside the more bawdy lines, is part of the wonder, for the graffiti read, "Entering the forest, God moves not the grass. Entering the water, God makes not a ripple."

Maybe that graffiti writer had a perverse and esoterically pornographic sense of humor, but I don't believe that. Standing there, I began to think that God entering human life seems to happen in ways that aren't very obvious, at least to most of us. And yet it is that "entering" that gives life the other dimension, or dimensions. It is this elusive, almost secretive entering—this quality to the Christmas event—which needs affirming, lest we miss something essential about what we are celebrating and, hopefully, living. Was it Mark Twain who said, "The greatest miracles happen just where people say, 'I don't see anything miraculous about that.' "?

So perhaps the real miracle—and mystery—of Christmas is a very human one. It is the mystery and the miracle of the specific, the human—as specific and human as each one of us, as the face you saw in the mirror this morning, as the old woman you passed on the stairs, as the children you almost tripped over on your way out of the subway or into the office, as the shoppers elbowing their way to the store counters, as the human faces and shapes and sizes and colors wandering the streets with you.

Isn't that what incarnation means, in part at least? God enters not only human life but our life—our time, our world. God is present with us, loving, working, nudging, nuzzling us here and now, but without making obvious ripples, or *any* ripples, unless you look with some imagination. God leaves tracks in the straw but they are faint— faint, but there for those who will discern. The graffiti writer is right: God enters and the grass doesn't move or the water ripple . . . much. But then, when you think about it, you realize that it really wasn't very obvious back in Jesus' time, or at his birth, for most people missed it then, too, and have missed it since, I suppose.

So probably we'll miss it, too. Not altogether, but in some crucial ways, just because we've been conditioned to dismiss mystery as only something we don't know "yet," rather than as something that is unknowable at all; and because we define miracles as something supernatural, and therefore impossible, since everything must have a natural explanation. But, "The greatest miracles happen just where people say, 'I don't see anything miraculous about that.' "

Back to the mirror and the streets! How *did* you get here at all, not just once but over and over? You, the specific constellation of cells, experiences, values, perceptions, thoughts, feelings, hopes, dreams, relationships that are you. And not only you, but other creatures. How did *they* get here, whoever they are? Births happen all the time, and we all get born, day by day, in a thousand strange ways: born, changed, made different, emerged or hurled to a new time, to a familiar yet always strange place and time. How does that happen? Things keep happening to us, in us, through us, around us: moments, gifts, ideas, encounters, words, feelings, choices, actions and reactions. How do they fit together? How do they bring us about? Where do they take us, and with whom? How does life happen "in the flesh" and what, finally, is life? Is it just breathing, just eating, just reproducing, just fact, just linear time?

Or perchance does life have something to do with that other

dimension toward which Christmas tugs us: incarnation, God entering human life without making a ripple or a roar (only a tremor and a whisper); God working, loving, scattering hints and possibilities in and among us. Maybe what Christmas celebrates, if we pay it half a mind (or heart), isn't God "back there" or "up there," but God *right here and now,* in surprising ways—very human, very specific and, therefore, very mysterious and miraculous ways.

And yet, it must never be forgotten that what makes the human—and the specific—miraculous and mysterious is God's presence in it, with us. The story is always about God, whether it be the Biblical story, the human story or the cosmic story. The story is finally and always about God and what God does with, in and for human beings, in spite of ourselves. Since, at best, we *do* pay it only half a mind, we usually miss, or at least *almost* miss, and always miss *most* of the ways the story is given to us.

I think it was Philip Melanchthon who said, "God calls, but he calls the willing ones." I'd rephrase that to say it's the willing ones who best *hear* the call. Maybe that is more than half of what faith is: hearing the call, the whispers and tremors, in and through all the hubbub and confusion of our common lives and common relationships. One of my beliefs is that everyone, every creature, is "willing" to some degree, and responds accordingly, partially, oft unknowingly and yet somehow unerringly. So in, and out of, all those varieties of responses, the miracles reside and the kingdom comes.

What I mean to be talking about, in untraditional language, is incarnation, God's presence with us in the earthiness and blunderings and incredible beauty of time and place and us. The point of incarnation, of Jesus the Christ, and the ongoing "with us" of God, is not only to make God believable to us, but to make us believable to ourselves, to each other, and to God. Just there—*there*—love begins to get born.

One or two more quick thoughts in this Epilogue. One is a question about *why* we miss the ways God is with us. For me the clue may be somewhere in a day like December 26th, when the celebration is over, and the turkey picked over; the gifts are put away, and the guests gone away. Often the feeling is that December 26th is a flat, grey day. I remember beginning to be aware of that feeling somewhere around my tenth or eleventh year. I think it was because my expectations of what would happen on Christmas day were so exaggerated, that the 26th was really doomed from the start.

But consider: isn't the point of the Christmas story that a *little* thing can be decisive? The story really isn't about angels and royal visitors; they were in the chorus, bit players. The central figure is a child; the main characters, a poor family; the occasion, an outback birth. The rest is sound and fury, diversion. God enters without a ripple, the grass doesn't move. The tracks are on the straw, but it takes a willing eye to trace them.

And yet . . . a little thing can tilt a teeter-totter from one side to the other; life can be like that, too. A small mid-course correction can completely change the destination of a space capsule or an airplane. Even so, seeing something just a little differently can sometimes shift the seer from misunderstanding to some understanding, from a one-dimensional life to at least a two-dimensional, maybe a multi-dimensional life. If one meaning of the word "salvation" is "wholeness," then the more dimensions we can experience in life, the more complete, or whole, life becomes.

So what Christmas—what faith—may be about is more like *transition* than resolution and "happily ever after." A transition occurs in a series of little changes—little births, as it were—little perceptions slowly, or perhaps rapidly, resulting in a shift of viewpoint, another way of seeing. A transition suggests a process that keeps going on, a process which involves trying something a little different because . . . well, because it's *possible.* And that it *is* possible is quite miracle enough—and more than enough mystery—especially when you begin to try to live the possibility, listen to it, be it, love it with a little imagination. So maybe the season really isn't so much like the *Hallelujah Chorus.* What's so wrong with a piccolo solo, or just whistling in the shower, or touching someone's hand, or wounds or . . . . what was Jesus about, anyway? Who was it said, "You don't get to the Christ without following Jesus"?

Now the last thought—or echoed whisper or ripple. For me, the most accurate way to touch on the mystery of the incarnation and the miracle of the human is through stories. A Jewish friend of mine once said, "We are liberated by the stories that read us." I find that persuasive. We *are* read by stories. So we become a story, or a thousand stories. Who knows all the strands that are woven to become the stories that read us; who knows the truths that resonate through the words, the scenes, the smells and tastes that enter us, take over our bones, our hearts and become our story? God knows, and that is enough.

One way or another—or a thousand other ways—we tell our stories and hear each other's stories. I wrote the stories in this book. They do not claim to know much. Maybe they can, or have, helped you to discover again what you already know inside, under the cobwebs, over in the corners, tucked away under all the layers of inattention and dust of indifference. Still, you do know . . .

But let me tell you a secret, a kind of parable. When I wrote these stories, each character took on his or her own personality, values, idiosyncracies. They became living beings for me, more than just inventions of my imagination, reflections of my story. They talked back to me. They wouldn't do things I wanted them to just because I wanted it. They had to consent. I had ideas; they rejected them. I proposed answers and solutions; they refused them. They insisted on their own way, and the stories felt most authentic when I gave in. These characters are demanding, stubborn, willful . . . and, to me, very beautiful. I got angry with them, despaired of them, tired of them. They taught me, stretched me, blessed me. And I love them. Very much. Very deeply. Now, do you suppose that is something of how it is with us and God, our Author, as it were? Is that kind of relationship something of what the story, our story . . . no, God's story, is about?

My final confession—and affirmation—is this: these stories, these characters, demanded of me (and do still) more than I had (or will ever have) to give. But in that, at least, I am unlike God who seems always to meet us where we are and go before us to where we're headed, even when we feel we've lost our bearings. So maybe Christmas, and these stories, answer our deepest question, "Where is God?," with another question which expresses my faith: "Where is God not?"

— Ted Loder

THE AUTHOR:
Ted Loder

Ted Loder has been called many names: "free-wheeling," "emotional," "provocative," "outrageous," "courageous." They're all true. As Senior Minister of one of Philadelphia's most unusual churches, the First United Methodist Church of Germantown (FUMCOG), he actively encourages openness to experiment and to change. He leads his church to the forefront of political activism and social concerns. FUMCOG is part of the Sanctuary movement for Central American refugees; Ted is Co-Founder and Chairman of the Board for the Metropolitan Collegiate Center (a program preparing disadvantaged youths for college and jobs); he is Co-Founder of Plowshares (a non-profit housing renovation corporation); Ted is also President of Metro-Ministries and a member of the Advisory Committee for Covenant House (a medical mission to depressed areas of the city). For many people, Ted Loder's mixture of scholarship (he's received his B.D. from Yale Divinity School and an honorary doctorate from Willamette University) and of creativity (the *National Observer* selected him as one of America's Outstanding Creative Preachers for writing and staging story and drama sermons) stimulates an emerging freedom to re-connect with the church, to re-explore beliefs, and to re-discover passion.

THE ARTIST:
Ed Kerns

Ed Kerns describes his paintings as a "personal embrace with eternal questions." Others have said that he dares "to explore . . . imagery that communicates instantly to the viewer." Currently Professor of Art and Chair of the Department at Lafayette College in Easton, Pennsylvania, Kerns is internationally known as an abstract painter. Represented by the Rosa Esman Gallery, his works have been exhibited in fifteen one-person shows in New York, as well as in Paris, London, and other principal European cities. Major art magazines, including *Art News, Artforum,* and *Arts,* along with *The New York Times* and *The Village Voice* have extensively reviewed his passionate, idiosyncratic style. Kerns, a graduate of Richmond Professional Institute (B.F.A.) and the Maryland Institute, College of Art (M.F.A.) is vitally interested in teaching and in creating. "The creative process," states Kerns, "is my continual attempt to re-define my way of seeing." His disclosure that his works are "not illustrations of preconceived ideas; they *are* the ideas" invites the viewer into personal uncharted realms of exploration, into the "embrace with eternal questions."

Other LuraMedia Publications

BANKSON, MARJORY ZOET

Braided Streams:
Esther and a Woman's Way of Growing

Seasons of Friendship:
Naomi and Ruth as a Pattern

"This Is My Body. . .":
Creativity, Clay, and Change

BOHLER, CAROLYN STAHL

Prayer on Wings: *A Search for Authentic Prayer*

**DOHERTY, DOROTHY ALBRACHT
and McNAMARA, MARY COLGAN**

Out of the Skin Into the Soul:
The Art of Aging

GEIGER, LURA JANE

and PATRICIA BACKMAN

Braided Streams Leader's Guide

and SUSAN TOBIAS

Seasons of Friendship Leader's Guide

GOODSON, WILLIAMSON (with Dale J.)

Re-Souled: *Spiritual Awakenings of a Psychiatrist
and his Patient in Alcohol Recovery*

JEVNE, RONNA FAY

It All Begins With Hope:
Patients, Caretakers, and the Bereaved Speak Out

and ALEXANDER LEVITAN

No Time for Nonsense:
Getting Well Against the Odds

KEIFFER, ANN

Gift of the Dark Angel: *A Woman's Journey
through Depression toward Wholeness*

LODER, TED

Eavesdropping on the Echoes:
Voices from the Old Testament

Guerrillas of Grace:
Prayers for the Battle

Tracks in the Straw:
Tales Spun from the Manger

Wrestling the Light:
Ache and Awe in the Human-Divine Struggle

MEYER, RICHARD C.

One Anothering:
Biblical Building Blocks for Small Groups

MILLETT, CRAIG

In God's Image:
Archetypes of Women in Scripture

PRICE, H.H.

Blackberry Season:
A Time to Mourn, A Time to Heal

RAFFA, JEAN BENEDICT

The Bridge to Wholeness:
A Feminine Alternative to the Hero Myth

Dream Theatres of the Soul:
*Empowering the Feminine through
Jungian Dreamwork*

SAURO, JOAN

Whole Earth Meditation:
Ecology for the Spirit

SCHAPER, DONNA

Stripping Down:
The Art of Spiritual Restoration

WEEMS, RENITA J.

Just a Sister Away: *A Womanist Vision
of Women's Relationships in the Bible*

I Asked for Intimacy: *Stories of Blessings,
Betrayals, and Birthings*

The Women's Series

BORTON, JOAN

Drawing from the Women's Well:
Reflections on the Life Passage of Menopause

CARTLEDGE-HAYES, MARY

To Love Delilah:
Claiming the Women of the Bible

DUERK, JUDITH

Circle of Stones:
Woman's Journey to Herself

I Sit Listening to the Wind:
Woman's Encounter within Herself

**O'HALLORAN, SUSAN and
DELATTRE, SUSAN**

The Woman Who Lost Her Heart:
A Tale of Reawakening

RUPP, JOYCE

The Star in My Heart:
Experiencing Sophia, Inner Wisdom

SCHNEIDER-AKER, KATHERINE

God's Forgotten Daughter:
*A Modern Midrash: What If
Jesus Had Been A Woman?*

LuraMedia, Inc. , 7060 Miramar Rd., Suite 104, San Diego, CA 92121
Call 1-800-FOR-LURA for information about bookstores or ordering.
Books for Healing and Hope, Balance and Justice.